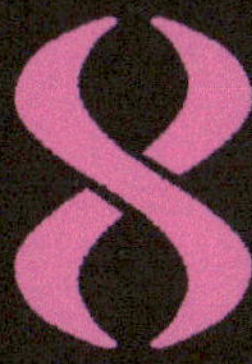

THE *SUPERVILLAIN* ORGANIZATION KNOWN AS THE *KORPS* HAS SPREAD THEIR INFLUENCE THROUGHOUT THE CONTINENT, CARVING OUT PLACES FOR THE LOST TO LIVE OUT OF SIGHT.

THE *TEXAS PROTECTORATE ASSEMBLY*, A CORPORATE-SPONSORED, SUPERPOWERED STATE LAW ENFORCEMENT AGENCY, HAS LAUNCHED AN OPERATION TO *ERADICATE* THE KORPS PRESENCE...STARTING IN THE CAPITAL, *AUSTIN*. THESE STATEWIDE ATTACKS ON KNOWN AND SUSPECTED KORPS SUPPORTERS AND ALLIES HAVE CAUGHT THEM OFF-GUARD.

NOW, VILLAINS ARE *SCRAMBLING* TO PROTECT THOSE THAT THE TPA HAS DEEMED UNDESIRABLE. BUT THE KORPS MUST WALK THE TIGHTROPE, LEST OTHER STATE AND NATIONAL HERO GROUPS CHOOSE TO GET INVOLVED, *IGNITING A FULL-SCALE WAR.*

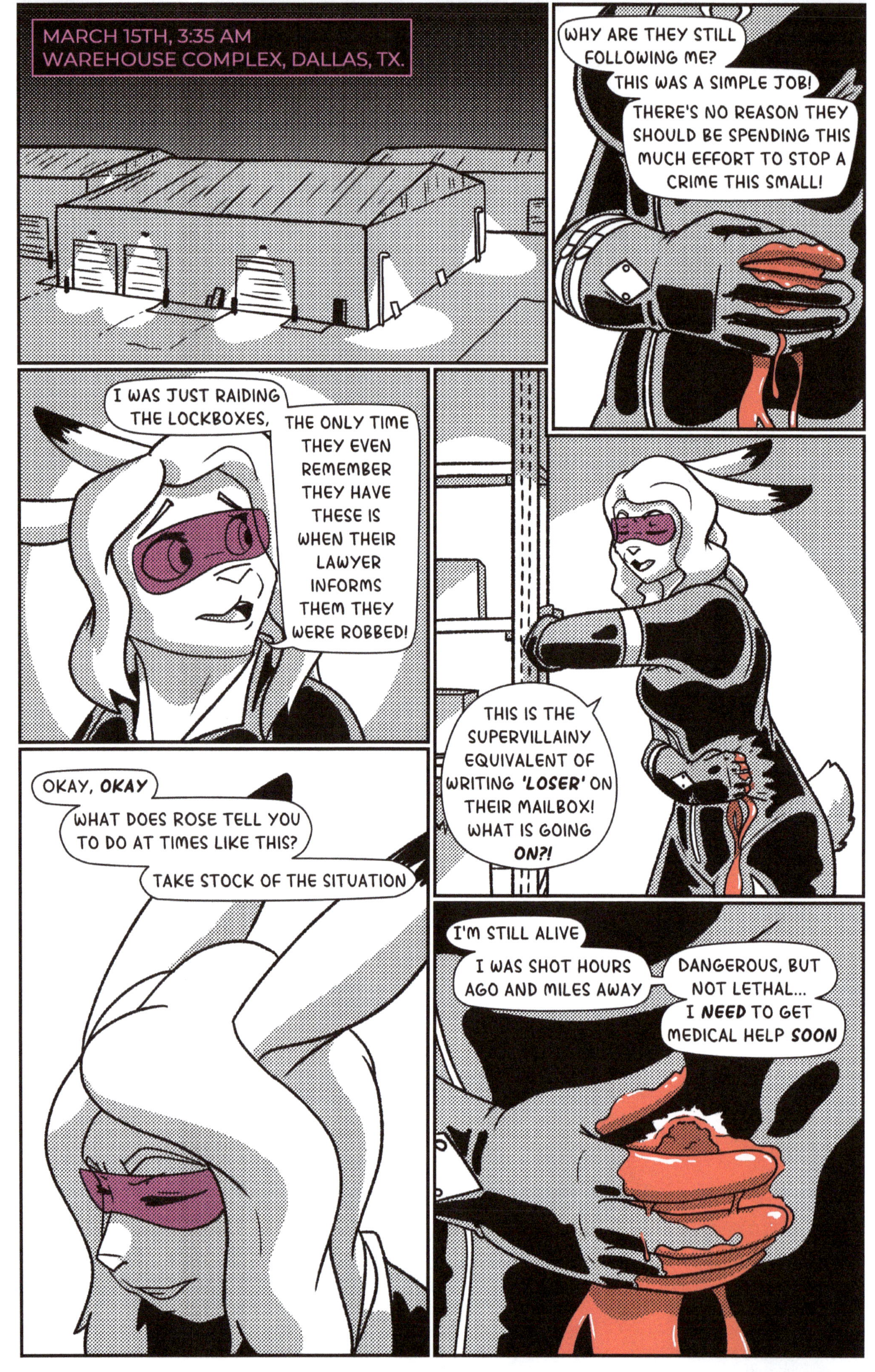

MARCH 15TH, 3:35 AM
WAREHOUSE COMPLEX, DALLAS, TX.

WHY ARE THEY STILL FOLLOWING ME?
THIS WAS A SIMPLE JOB!
THERE'S NO REASON THEY SHOULD BE SPENDING THIS MUCH EFFORT TO STOP A CRIME THIS SMALL!

I WAS JUST RAIDING THE LOCKBOXES,
THE ONLY TIME THEY EVEN REMEMBER THEY HAVE THESE IS WHEN THEIR LAWYER INFORMS THEM THEY WERE ROBBED!

THIS IS THE SUPERVILLAINY EQUIVALENT OF WRITING 'LOSER' ON THEIR MAILBOX! WHAT IS GOING ON?!

OKAY, OKAY
WHAT DOES ROSE TELL YOU TO DO AT TIMES LIKE THIS?
TAKE STOCK OF THE SITUATION

I'M STILL ALIVE
I WAS SHOT HOURS AGO AND MILES AWAY
DANGEROUS, BUT NOT LETHAL...
I NEED TO GET MEDICAL HELP SOON

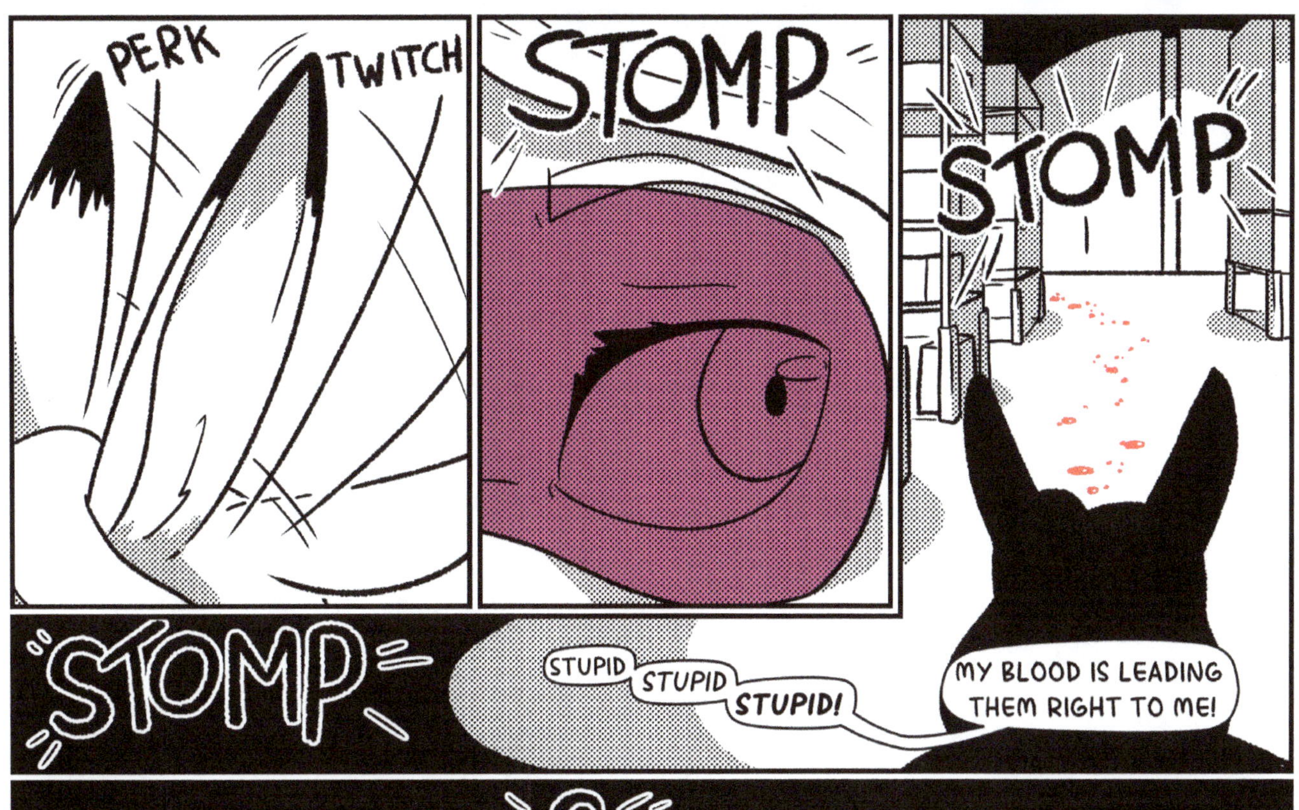

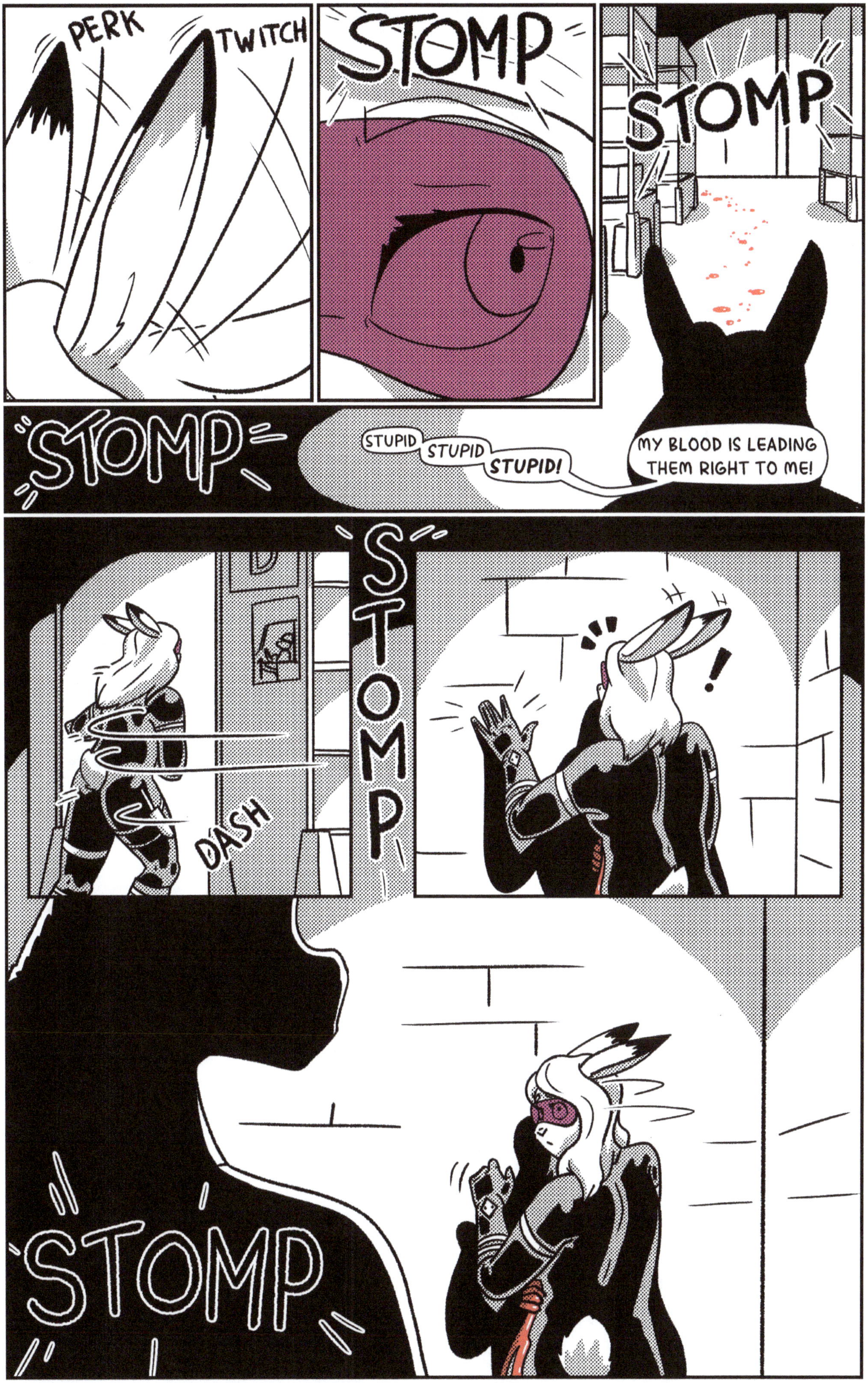

PERK
TWITCH
STOMP
STOMP
STOMP
STUPID STUPID STUPID!
MY BLOOD IS LEADING THEM RIGHT TO ME!

STOMP
DASH
STOMP
STOMP

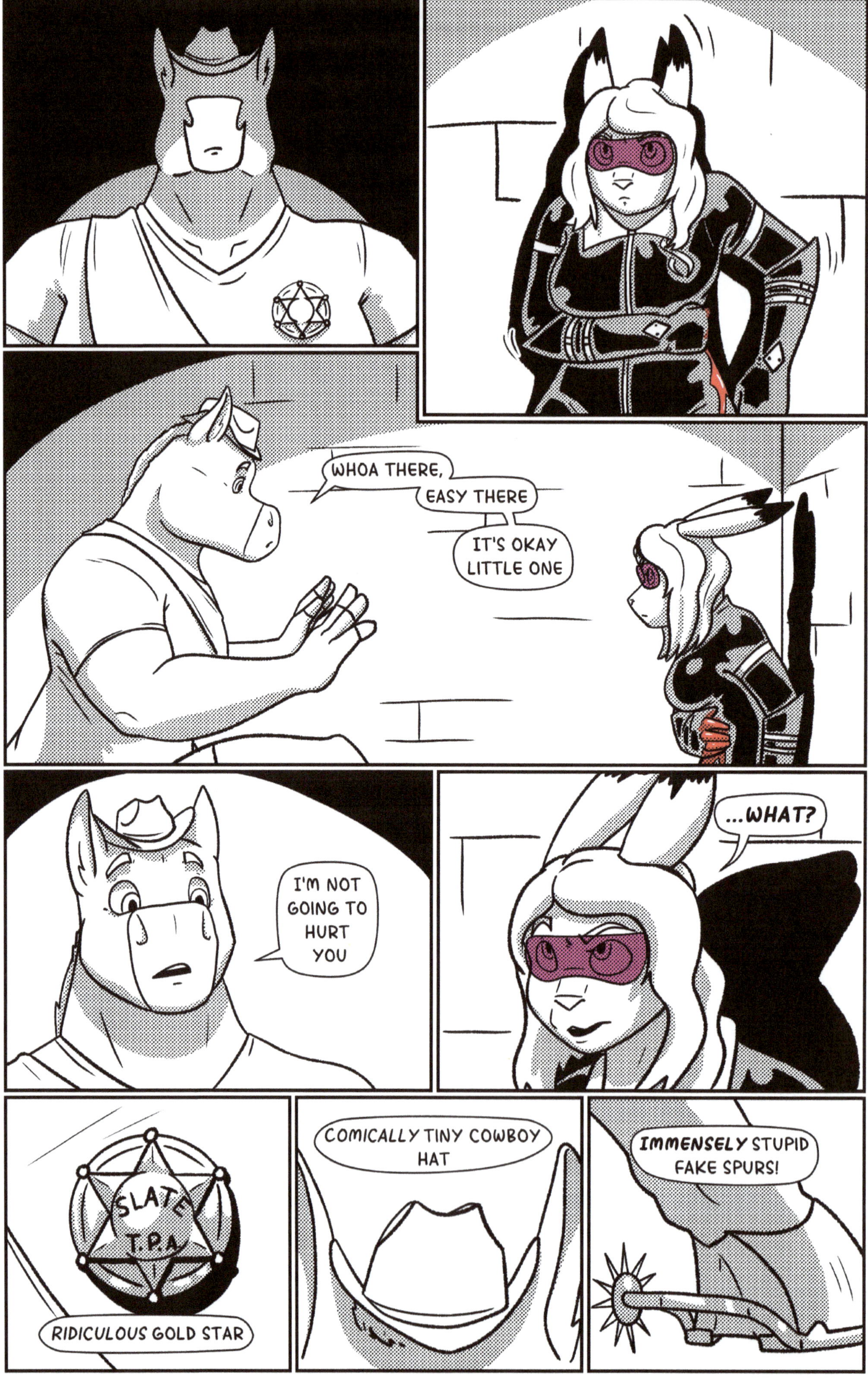

WHOA THERE, EASY THERE
IT'S OKAY LITTLE ONE
I'M NOT GOING TO HURT YOU
...WHAT?
SLATE T.P.A.
RIDICULOUS GOLD STAR
COMICALLY TINY COWBOY HAT
IMMENSELY STUPID FAKE SPURS!

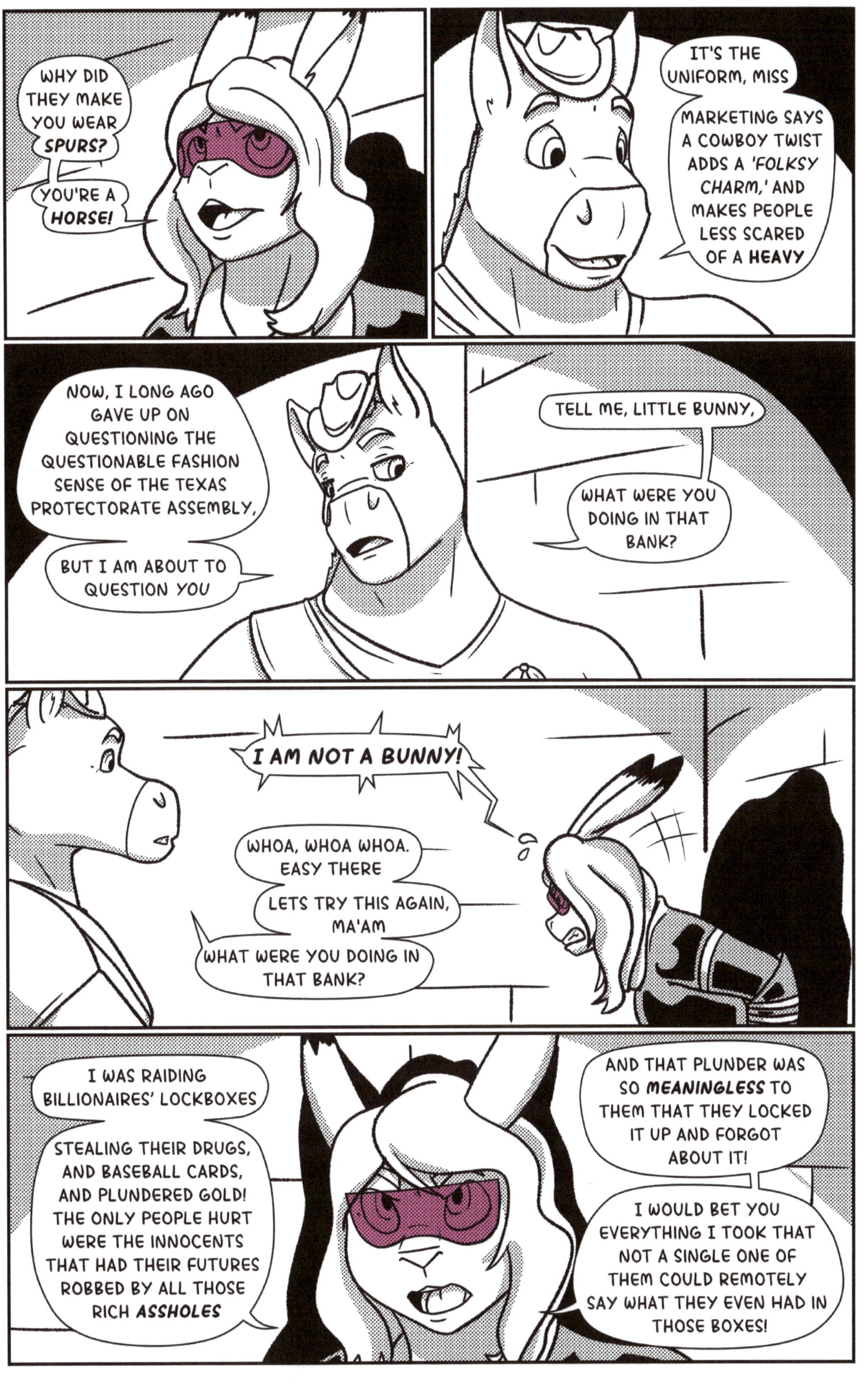

WHY DID THEY MAKE YOU WEAR SPURS?
YOU'RE A HORSE!
IT'S THE UNIFORM, MISS
MARKETING SAYS A COWBOY TWIST ADDS A 'FOLKSY CHARM,' AND MAKES PEOPLE LESS SCARED OF A HEAVY
NOW, I LONG AGO GAVE UP ON QUESTIONING THE QUESTIONABLE FASHION SENSE OF THE TEXAS PROTECTORATE ASSEMBLY,
BUT I AM ABOUT TO QUESTION YOU
TELL ME, LITTLE BUNNY,
WHAT WERE YOU DOING IN THAT BANK?
I AM NOT A BUNNY!
WHOA, WHOA WHOA. EASY THERE
LETS TRY THIS AGAIN, MA'AM
WHAT WERE YOU DOING IN THAT BANK?
I WAS RAIDING BILLIONAIRES' LOCKBOXES
STEALING THEIR DRUGS, AND BASEBALL CARDS, AND PLUNDERED GOLD! THE ONLY PEOPLE HURT WERE THE INNOCENTS THAT HAD THEIR FUTURES ROBBED BY ALL THOSE RICH ASSHOLES
AND THAT PLUNDER WAS SO MEANINGLESS TO THEM THAT THEY LOCKED IT UP AND FORGOT ABOUT IT!
I WOULD BET YOU EVERYTHING I TOOK THAT NOT A SINGLE ONE OF THEM COULD REMOTELY SAY WHAT THEY EVEN HAD IN THOSE BOXES!

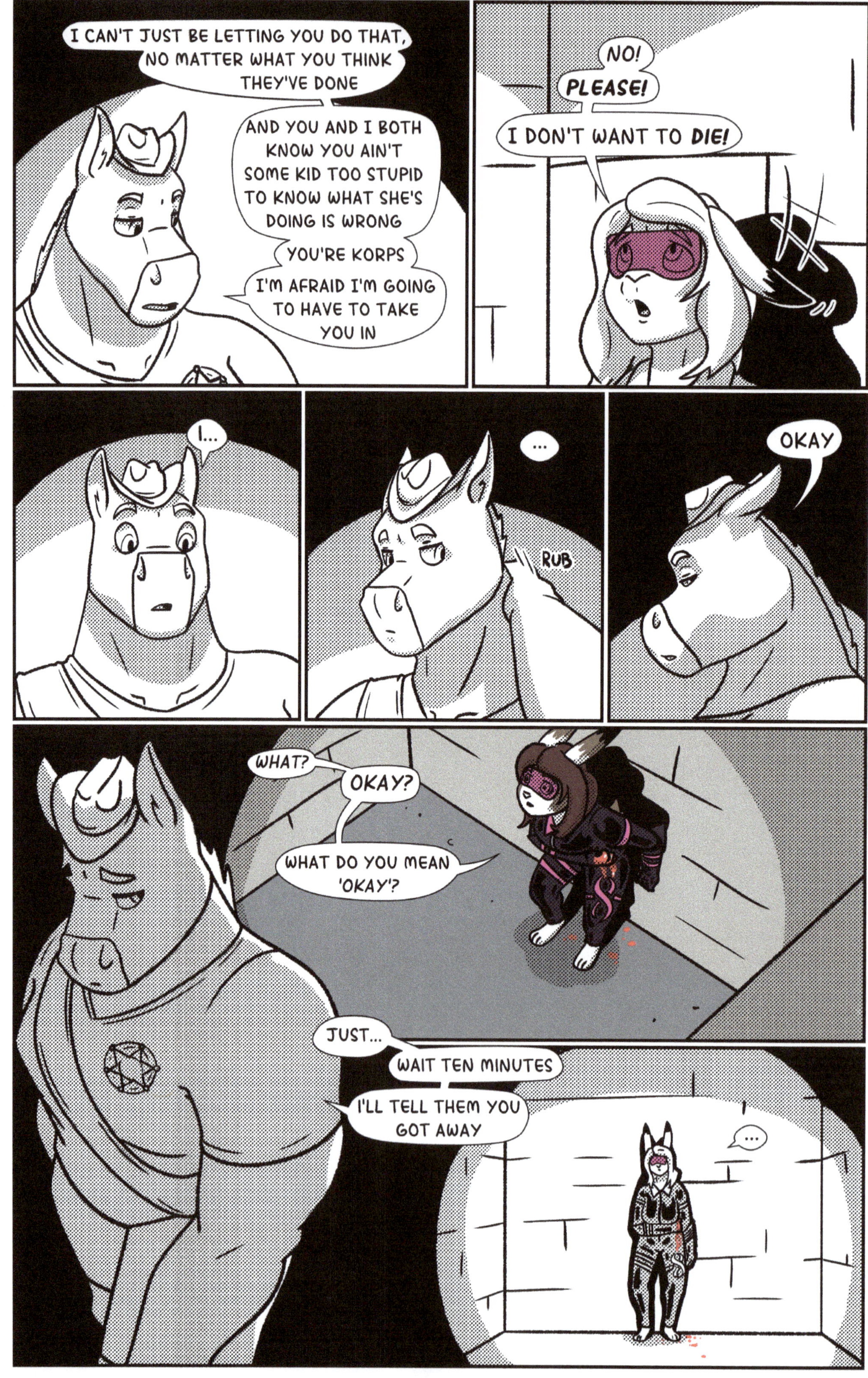

I CAN'T JUST BE LETTING YOU DO THAT, NO MATTER WHAT YOU THINK THEY'VE DONE
AND YOU AND I BOTH KNOW YOU AIN'T SOME KID TOO STUPID TO KNOW WHAT SHE'S DOING IS WRONG
YOU'RE KORPS
I'M AFRAID I'M GOING TO HAVE TO TAKE YOU IN
NO! PLEASE!
I DON'T WANT TO DIE!
I...
...
RUB
OKAY
WHAT?
OKAY?
WHAT DO YOU MEAN 'OKAY'?
JUST...
WAIT TEN MINUTES
I'LL TELL THEM YOU GOT AWAY
...

SURFACE RUPTURE

FOUR DAYS LATER - RIV BASE - BENEATH AUSTIN, TX
HEY, CARM! CAN YOU KEEP ME UPDATED ON HOW VOLTA'S DOING OVER COMMS?
?
VOLTA? SURE, BUT WHY THE SUDDEN INTEREST?
YOU MAKING EYES AT MY GIRLFRIEND, ELLE?
NO, NO— JUST TRYING TO STAY...
wink!
CURRENT...

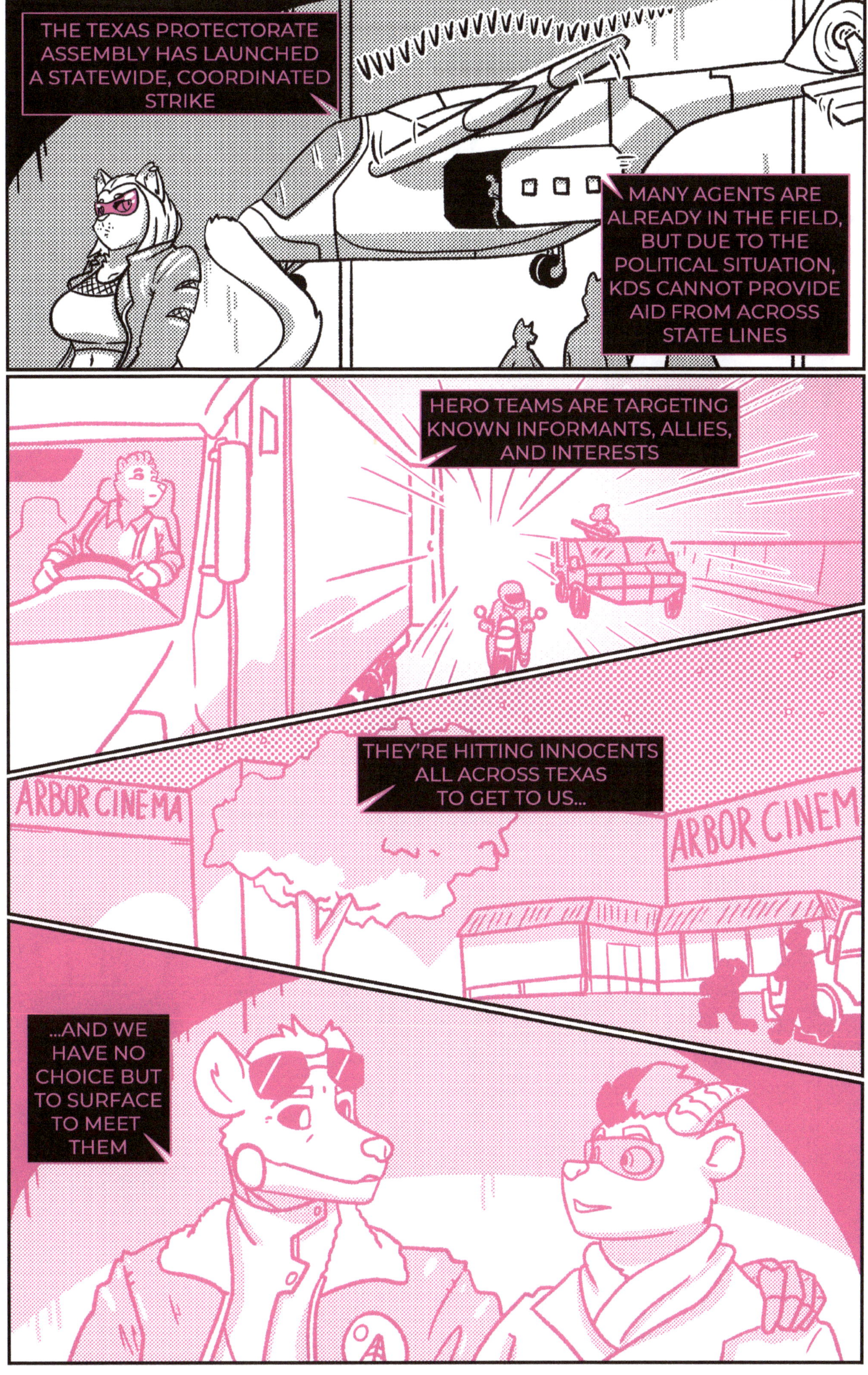

THE TEXAS PROTECTORATE ASSEMBLY HAS LAUNCHED A STATEWIDE, COORDINATED STRIKE
MANY AGENTS ARE ALREADY IN THE FIELD, BUT DUE TO THE POLITICAL SITUATION, KDS CANNOT PROVIDE AID FROM ACROSS STATE LINES
HERO TEAMS ARE TARGETING KNOWN INFORMANTS, ALLIES, AND INTERESTS
THEY'RE HITTING INNOCENTS ALL ACROSS TEXAS TO GET TO US...
ARBOR CINEMA
ARBOR CINEM
...AND WE HAVE NO CHOICE BUT TO SURFACE TO MEET THEM

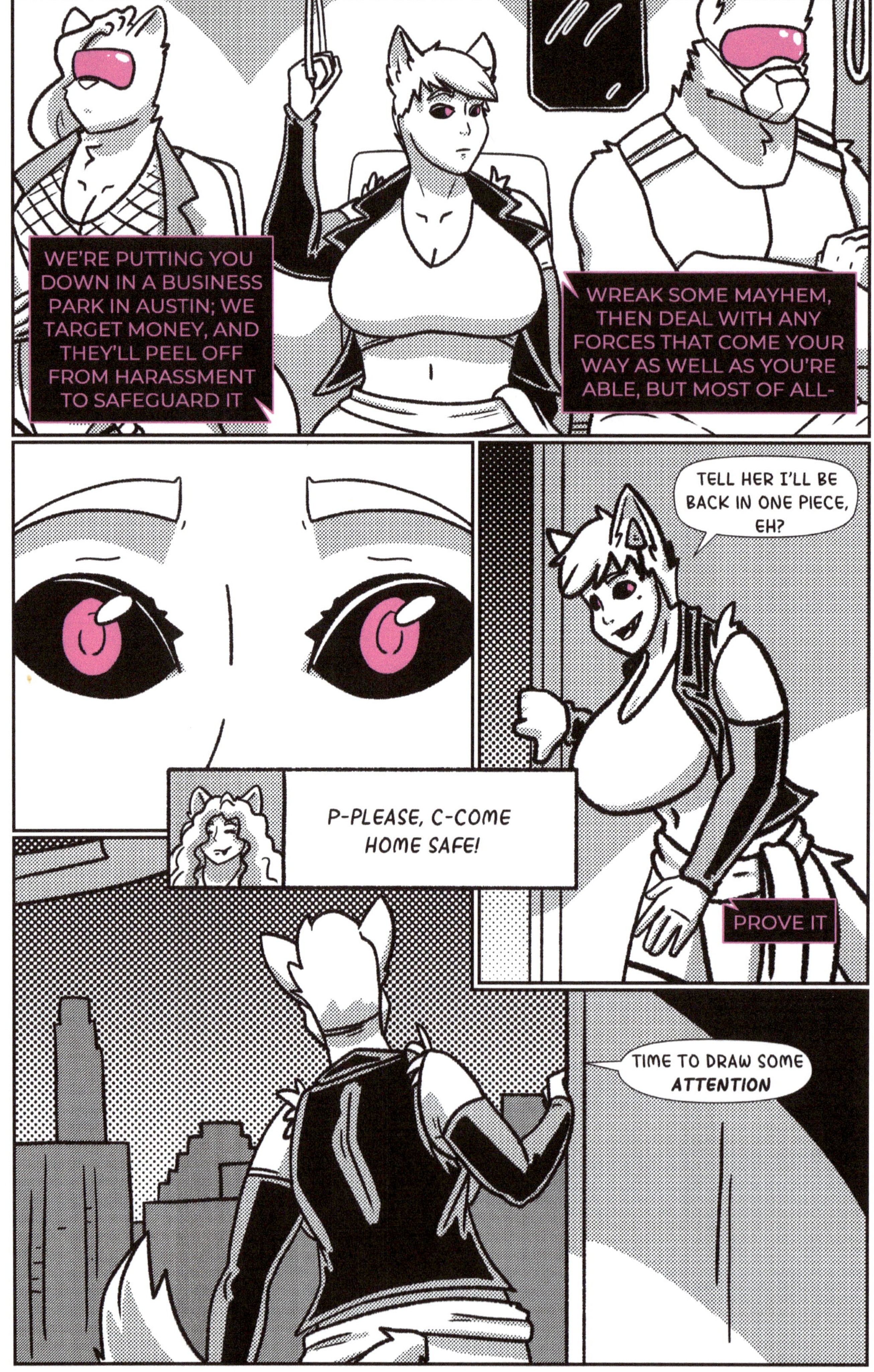

WE'RE PUTTING YOU DOWN IN A BUSINESS PARK IN AUSTIN; WE TARGET MONEY, AND THEY'LL PEEL OFF FROM HARASSMENT TO SAFEGUARD IT
WREAK SOME MAYHEM, THEN DEAL WITH ANY FORCES THAT COME YOUR WAY AS WELL AS YOU'RE ABLE, BUT MOST OF ALL-
TELL HER I'LL BE BACK IN ONE PIECE, EH?
P-PLEASE, C-COME HOME SAFE!
PROVE IT
TIME TO DRAW SOME ATTENTION

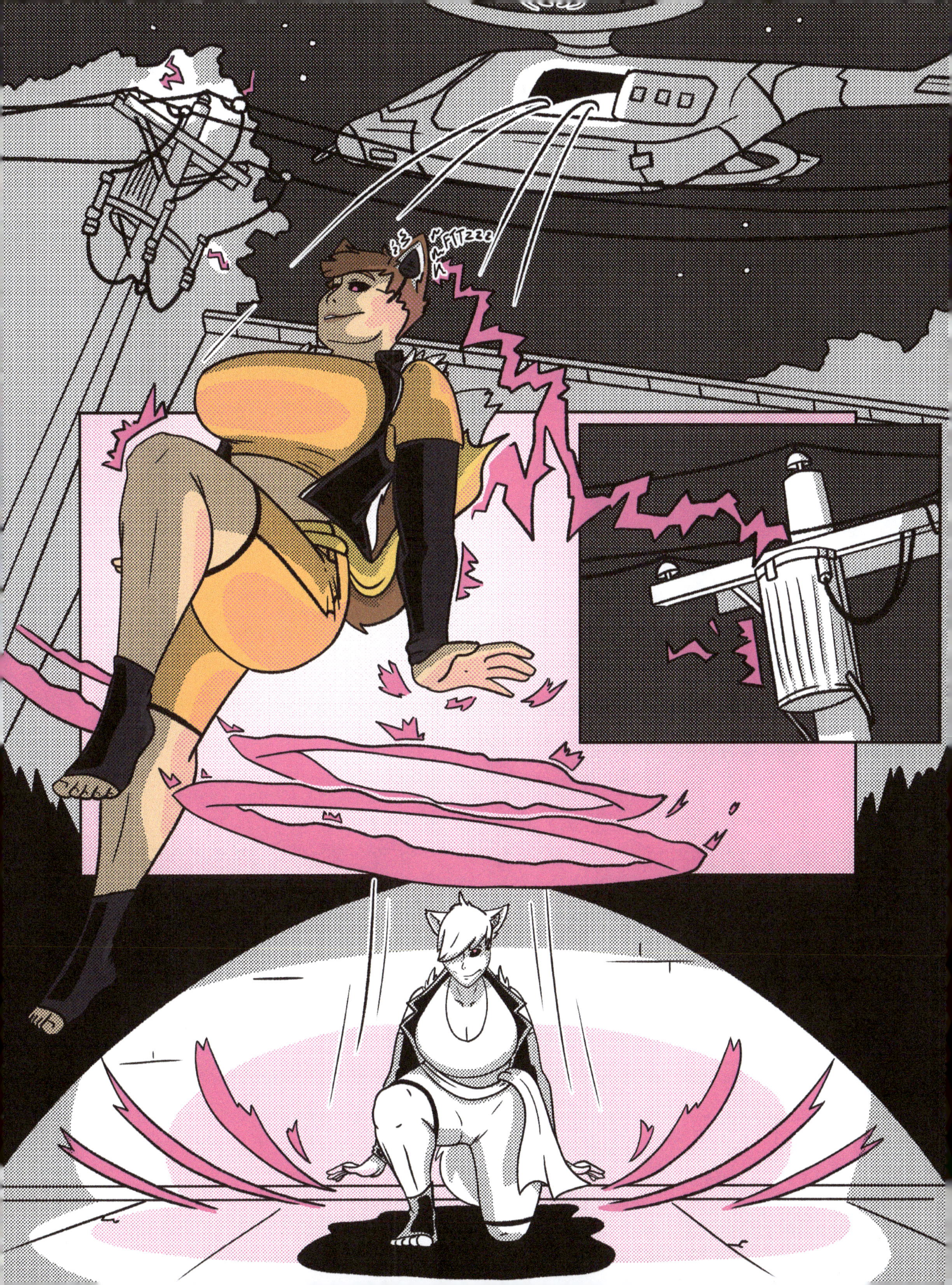
FTZZZ

ELSEWHERE IN AUSTIN, ON A DISTINCTLY EMPTY ROOFTOP
YOU'RE RECON, MABEL
FOLLOW ORDERS, MABEL
DON'T BE RECKLESS, MABEL
MONITOR YOUR QUADRANT, MABEL

! MOVEMENT DETECTED
...WAIT

SIGH

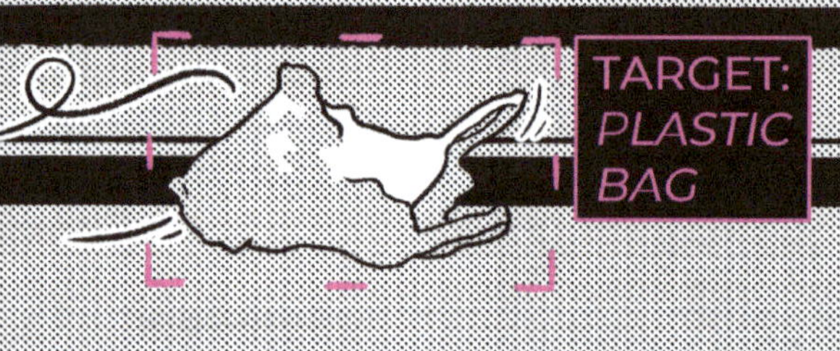

TARGET: PLASTIC BAG

THE QUADRANT WHERE NOTHING IS HAPPENING!
NEVER GET TO HAVE ANY FUN...
WELL WE DIDN'T KNOW THAT AHEAD OF TIME, MABES. JUST KEEP AN EYE OUT FOR CIVILIANS IN TROUBLE, OR SUSPICIOUS MOVEMENTS

ALL THE CAPES AND COPS ARE BUSY PLAYING WITH EVERYONE ELSE
RELLY, I'M TRYING TO BE A TEAM PLAYER HERE, BUT I FEEL LIKE I'M BEING UNDERUTILISED...

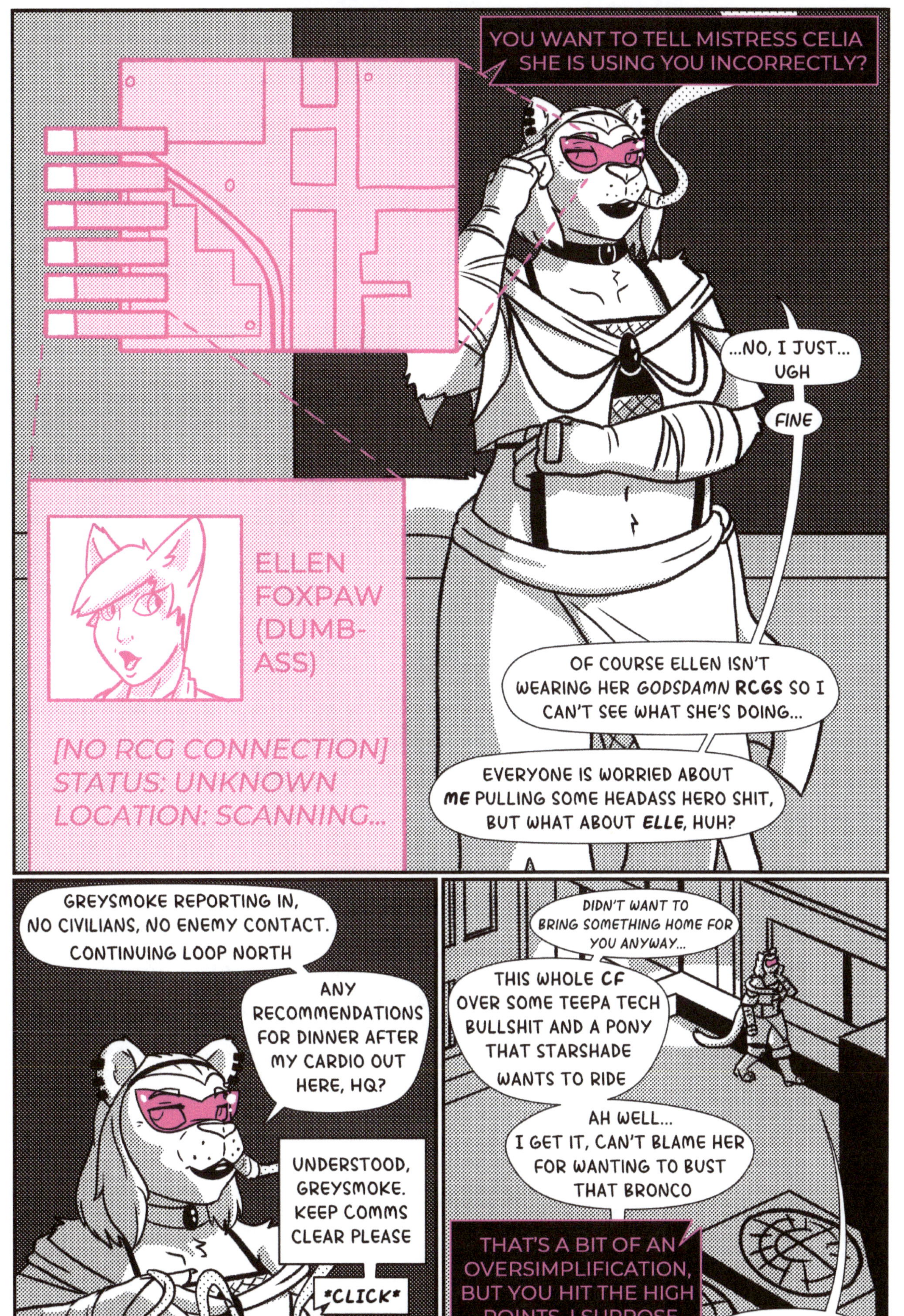
YOU WANT TO TELL MISTRESS CELIA SHE IS USING YOU INCORRECTLY?
...NO, I JUST... UGH
FINE
ELLEN FOXPAW (DUMB-ASS)
[NO RCG CONNECTION] STATUS: UNKNOWN LOCATION: SCANNING...
OF COURSE ELLEN ISN'T WEARING HER GODSDAMN RCGS SO I CAN'T SEE WHAT SHE'S DOING...
EVERYONE IS WORRIED ABOUT ME PULLING SOME HEADASS HERO SHIT, BUT WHAT ABOUT ELLE, HUH?
GREYSMOKE REPORTING IN, NO CIVILIANS, NO ENEMY CONTACT. CONTINUING LOOP NORTH
ANY RECOMMENDATIONS FOR DINNER AFTER MY CARDIO OUT HERE, HQ?
UNDERSTOOD, GREYSMOKE. KEEP COMMS CLEAR PLEASE
CLICK
DIDN'T WANT TO BRING SOMETHING HOME FOR YOU ANYWAY...
THIS WHOLE CF OVER SOME TEEPA TECH BULLSHIT AND A PONY THAT STARSHADE WANTS TO RIDE
AH WELL... I GET IT, CAN'T BLAME HER FOR WANTING TO BUST THAT BRONCO
THAT'S A BIT OF AN OVERSIMPLIFICATION, BUT YOU HIT THE HIGH POINTS, I SUPPOSE
THAT'S ME! NEW CALLSIGN IS 'HIGHLIGHT REEL'!

WAIT
PULL UP THE MAP AGAIN
WHERE'S ELLEN?
HER COMMS WENT OUT
SHE DECIDED THAT PUNNING INTO VOLTA WAS THE INTELLIGENT CHOICE, AND HER GEAR WASN'T EQUIPPED TO HANDLE IT
HA!
WELL THAT'LL BE...
FUN...
WAIT
SHE'S PRETENDING TO BE VOLTA?
MHMM, IN A CITY FULL OF...
WAIT
NO!
NO
NO
NO
NO
NO
NO!
RELLY!
LAST KNOWN LOCATION, NOW!
FLICK!

-POOF!-
PLEASE LET ME BE WRONG
PUFF
POOF
!
PLEASE LET ME BE PARANOID
FWOOSH
FWOOF
?
PUFF
GODS PLEASE...
NOT HIM

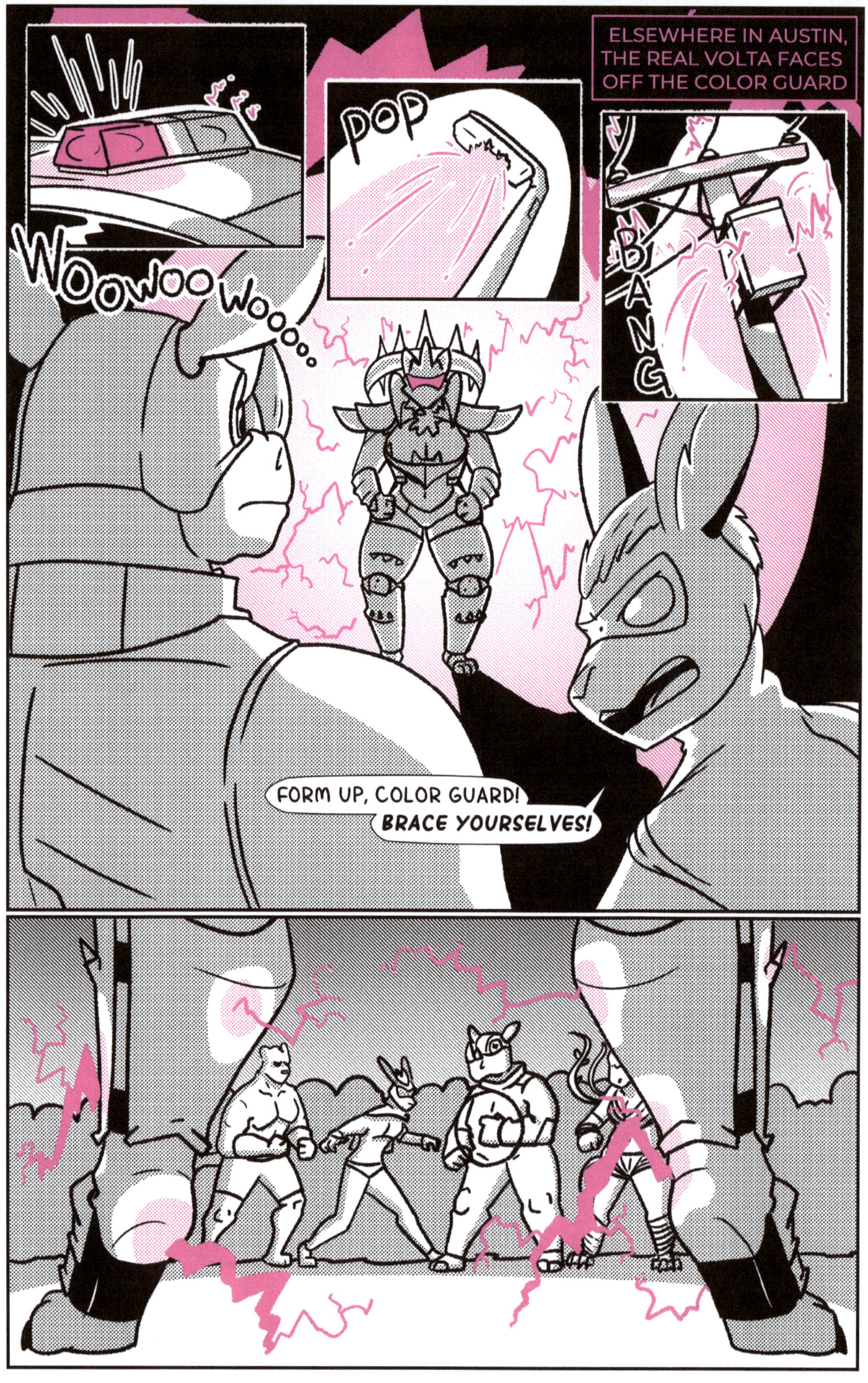

ELSEWHERE IN AUSTIN, THE REAL VOLTA FACES OFF THE COLOR GUARD
POP
BANG
WOOWOOWOOO...
FORM UP, COLOR GUARD!
BRACE YOURSELVES!

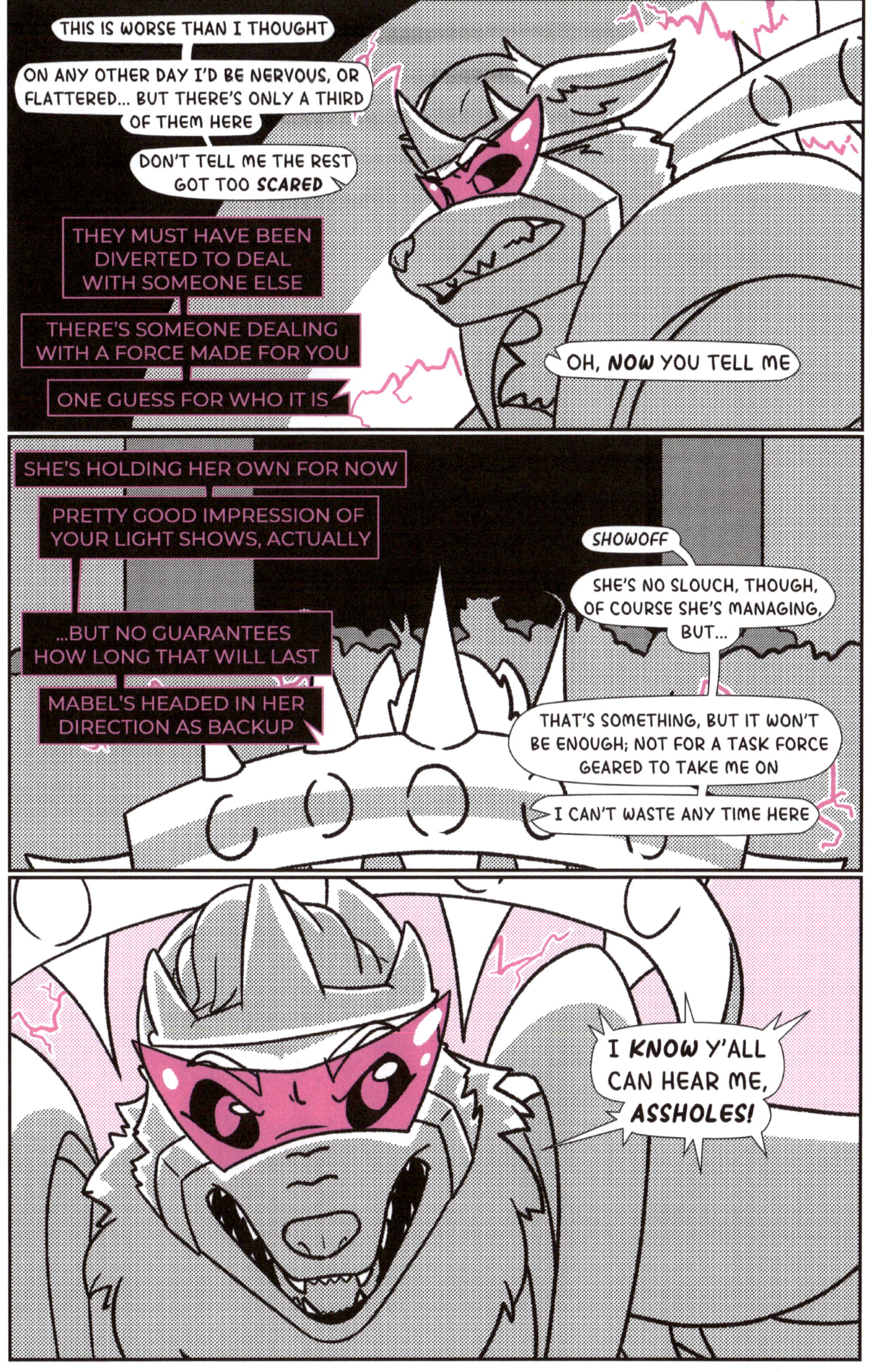

THIS IS WORSE THAN I THOUGHT
ON ANY OTHER DAY I'D BE NERVOUS, OR FLATTERED... BUT THERE'S ONLY A THIRD OF THEM HERE
DON'T TELL ME THE REST GOT TOO SCARED
THEY MUST HAVE BEEN DIVERTED TO DEAL WITH SOMEONE ELSE
THERE'S SOMEONE DEALING WITH A FORCE MADE FOR YOU
ONE GUESS FOR WHO IT IS
OH, NOW YOU TELL ME
SHE'S HOLDING HER OWN FOR NOW
PRETTY GOOD IMPRESSION OF YOUR LIGHT SHOWS, ACTUALLY
...BUT NO GUARANTEES HOW LONG THAT WILL LAST
MABEL'S HEADED IN HER DIRECTION AS BACKUP
SHOWOFF
SHE'S NO SLOUCH, THOUGH, OF COURSE SHE'S MANAGING, BUT...
THAT'S SOMETHING, BUT IT WON'T BE ENOUGH; NOT FOR A TASK FORCE GEARED TO TAKE ME ON
I CAN'T WASTE ANY TIME HERE
I KNOW Y'ALL CAN HEAR ME, ASSHOLES!

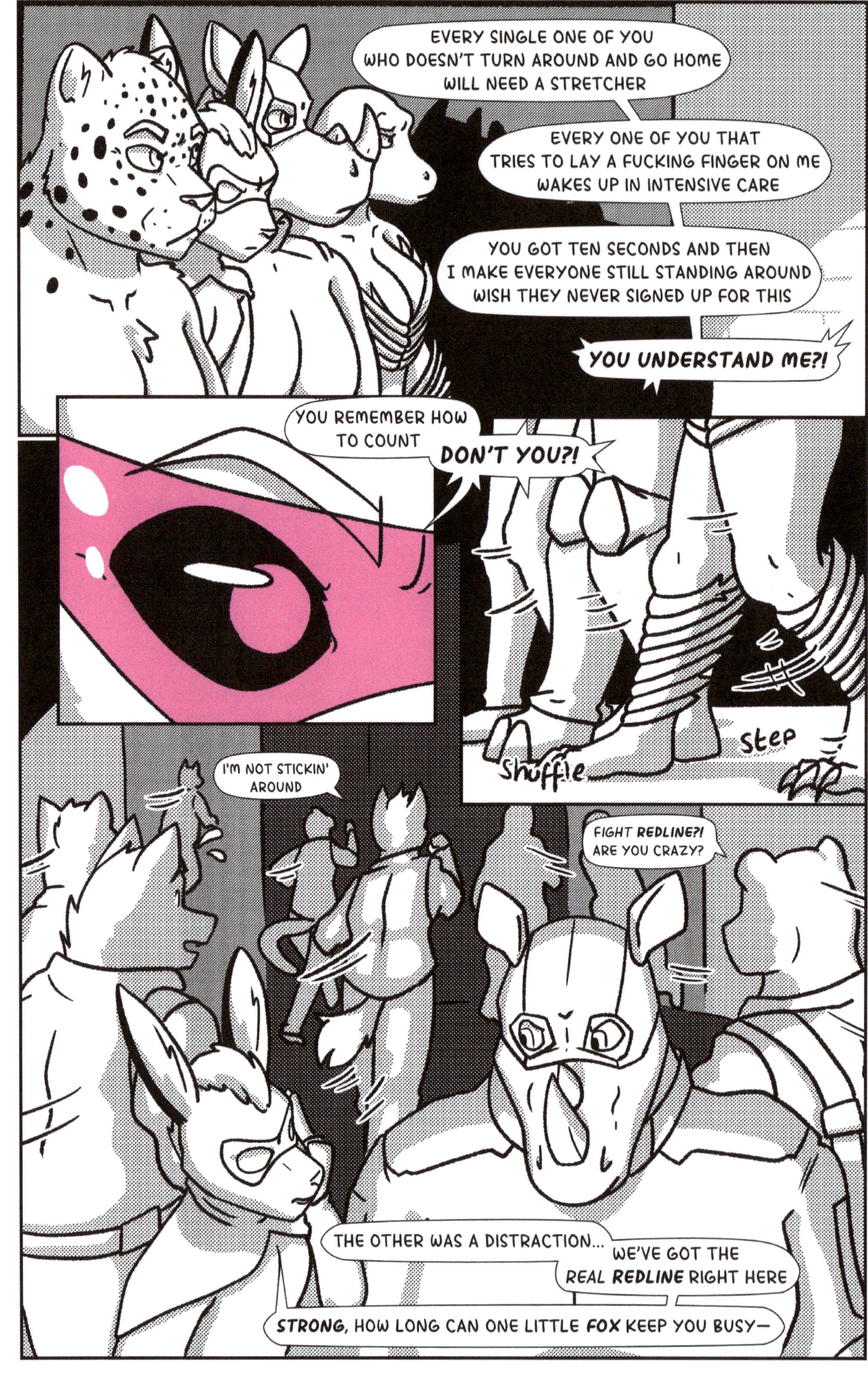

EVERY SINGLE ONE OF YOU WHO DOESN'T TURN AROUND AND GO HOME WILL NEED A STRETCHER
EVERY ONE OF YOU THAT TRIES TO LAY A FUCKING FINGER ON ME WAKES UP IN INTENSIVE CARE
YOU GOT TEN SECONDS AND THEN I MAKE EVERYONE STILL STANDING AROUND WISH THEY NEVER SIGNED UP FOR THIS
YOU UNDERSTAND ME?!
YOU REMEMBER HOW TO COUNT
DON'T YOU?!
shuffle
step
I'M NOT STICKIN' AROUND
FIGHT REDLINE?! ARE YOU CRAZY?
THE OTHER WAS A DISTRACTION... WE'VE GOT THE REAL REDLINE RIGHT HERE
STRONG, HOW LONG CAN ONE LITTLE FOX KEEP YOU BUSY—

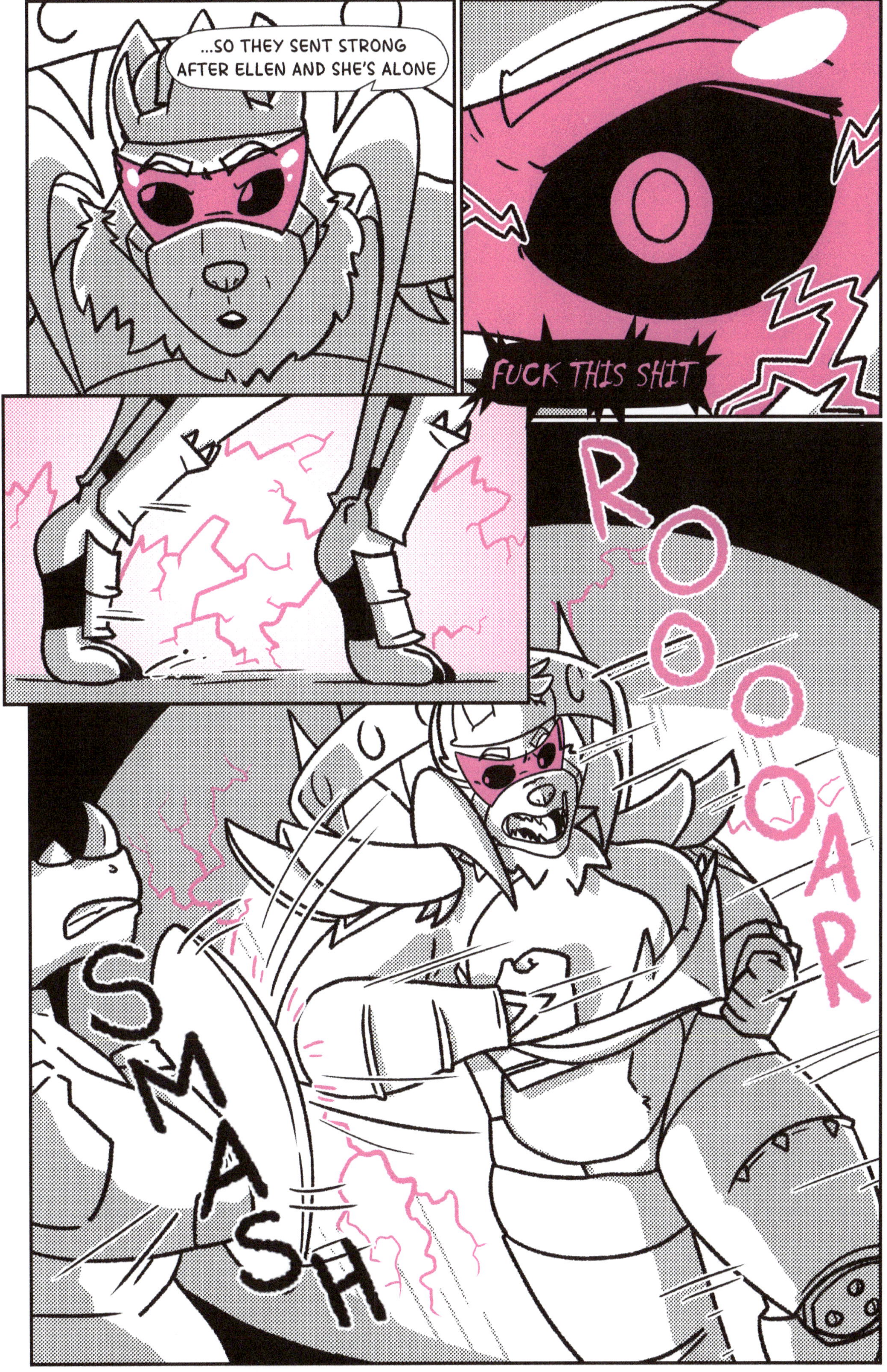
...SO THEY SENT STRONG AFTER ELLEN AND SHE'S ALONE
FUCK THIS SHIT
ROOOOOAR
SMASH

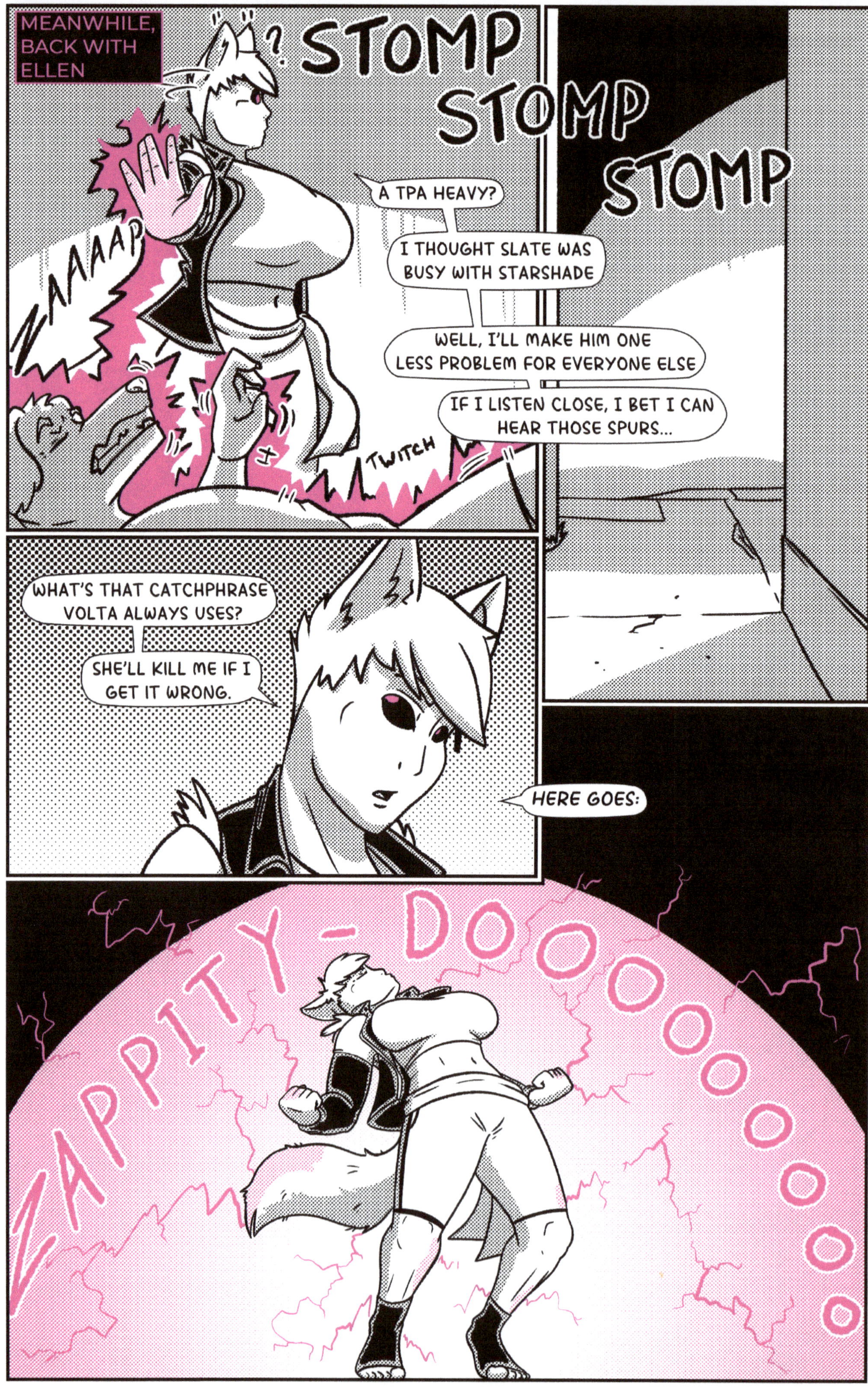

MEANWHILE, BACK WITH ELLEN
STOMP
STOMP
STOMP
ZZAAAAP
TWITCH
A TPA HEAVY?
I THOUGHT SLATE WAS BUSY WITH STARSHADE
WELL, I'LL MAKE HIM ONE LESS PROBLEM FOR EVERYONE ELSE
IF I LISTEN CLOSE, I BET I CAN HEAR THOSE SPURS...
WHAT'S THAT CATCHPHRASE VOLTA ALWAYS USES?
SHE'LL KILL ME IF I GET IT WRONG.
HERE GOES:
ZAPPITY-DOOOOOOOOO

Ooooooh-no...
CRUNCH
OH... FUCKADOODLE
THAT'S WHY I COULDN'T HEAR THAT JINGLE JANGLE JINGLE!
HEY, UH,
HQ?!!
...

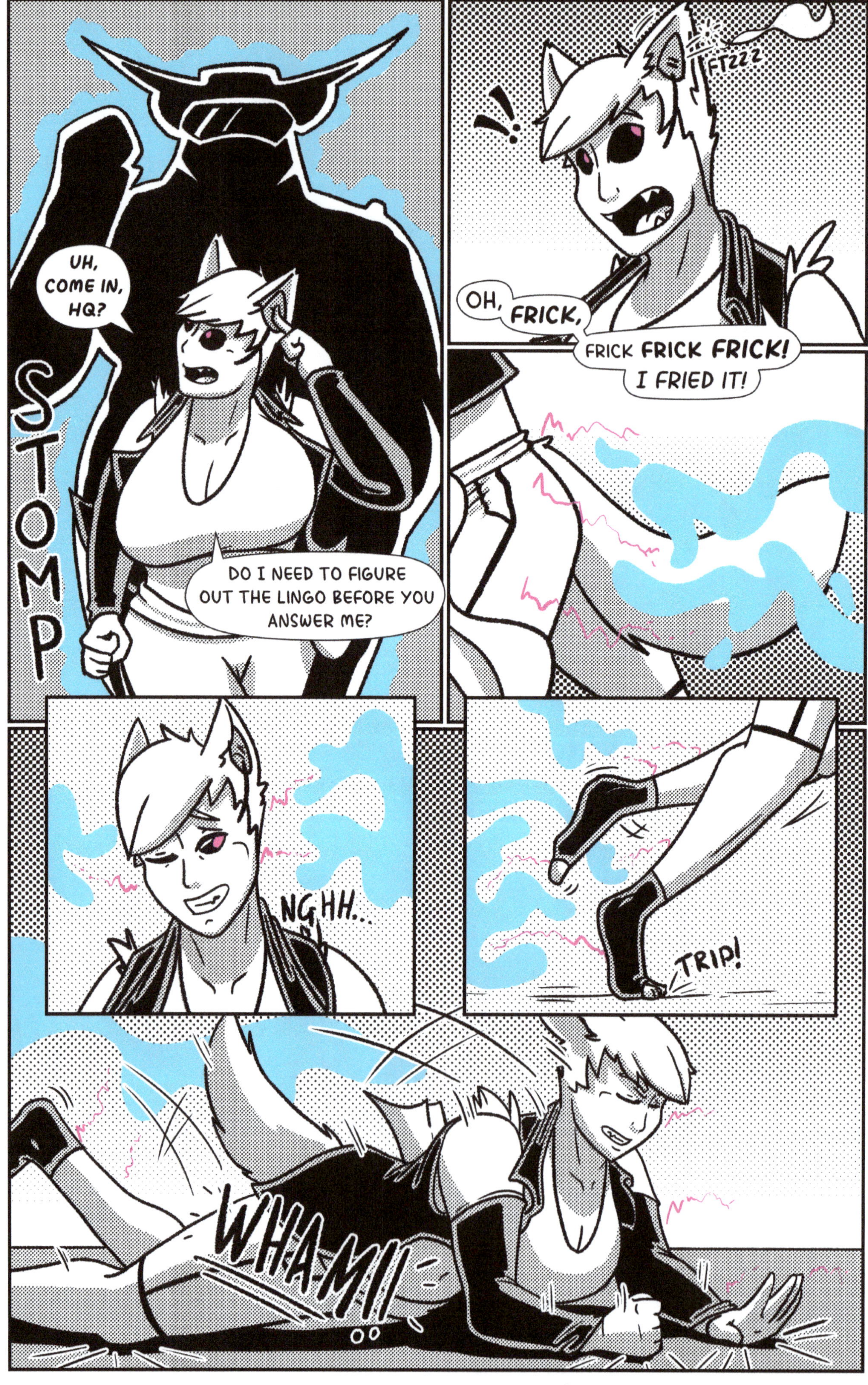

UH, COME IN, HQ?
STOMP
DO I NEED TO FIGURE OUT THE LINGO BEFORE YOU ANSWER ME?
FTZZZ
OH, FRICK, FRICK FRICK FRICK! I FRIED IT!
NGHH...
TRIP!
WHAM!!

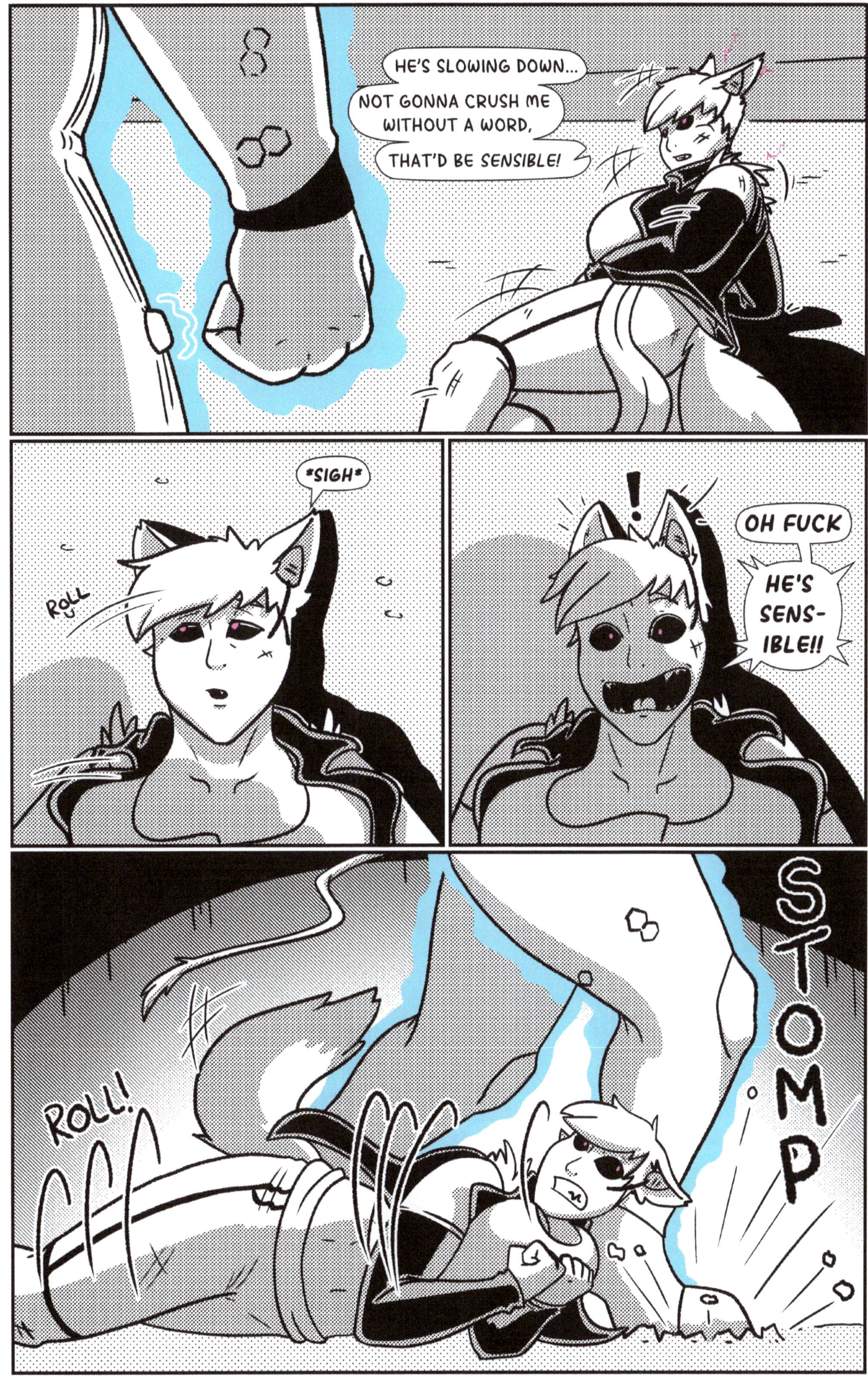

HE'S SLOWING DOWN...
NOT GONNA CRUSH ME WITHOUT A WORD, THAT'D BE SENSIBLE!
SIGH
ROLL
!
OH FUCK
HE'S SENS- IBLE!!
ROLL!!
STOMP

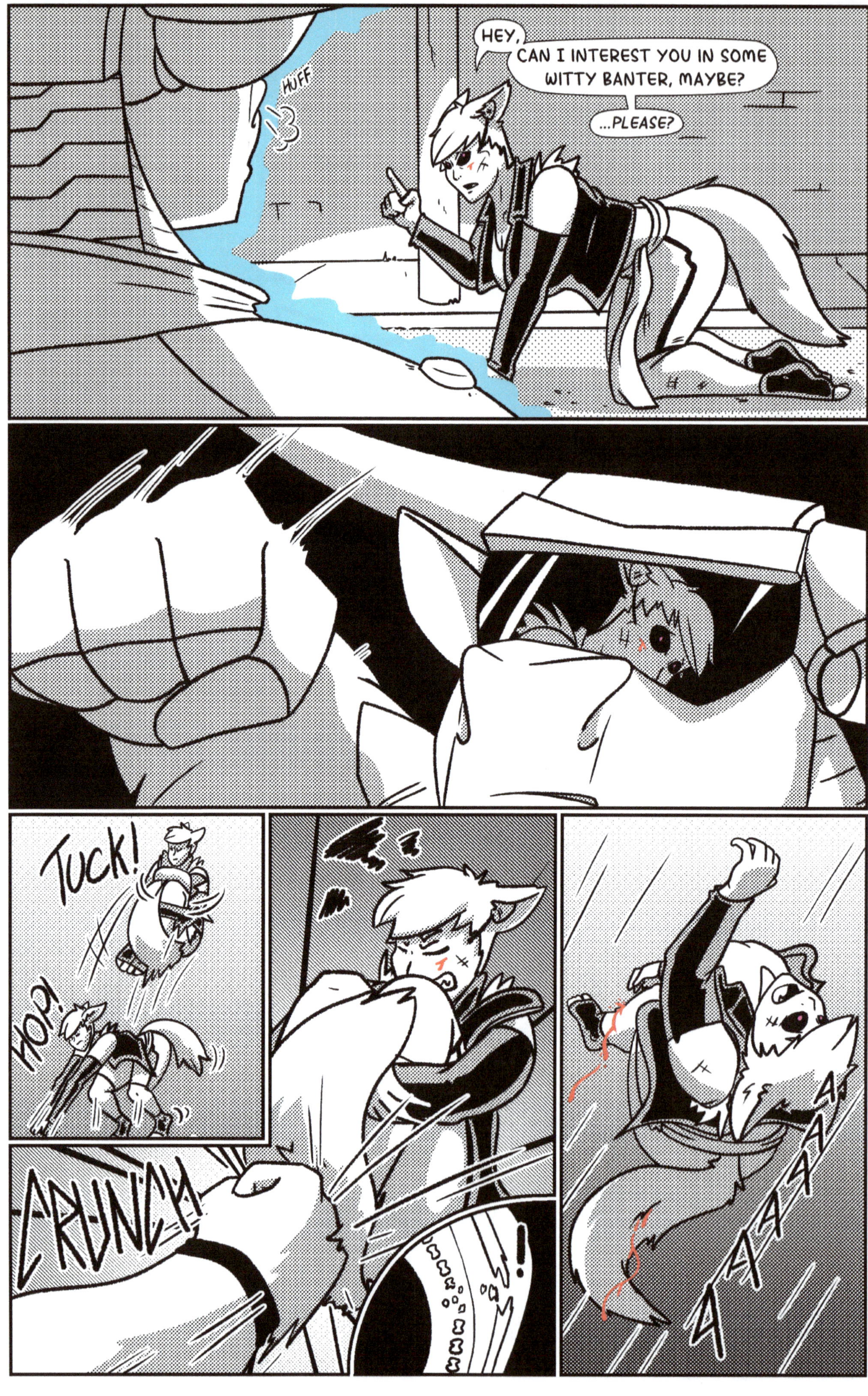

HUFF
HEY,
CAN I INTEREST YOU IN SOME WITTY BANTER, MAYBE?
...PLEASE?
TUCK!
HOP!
CRUNCH

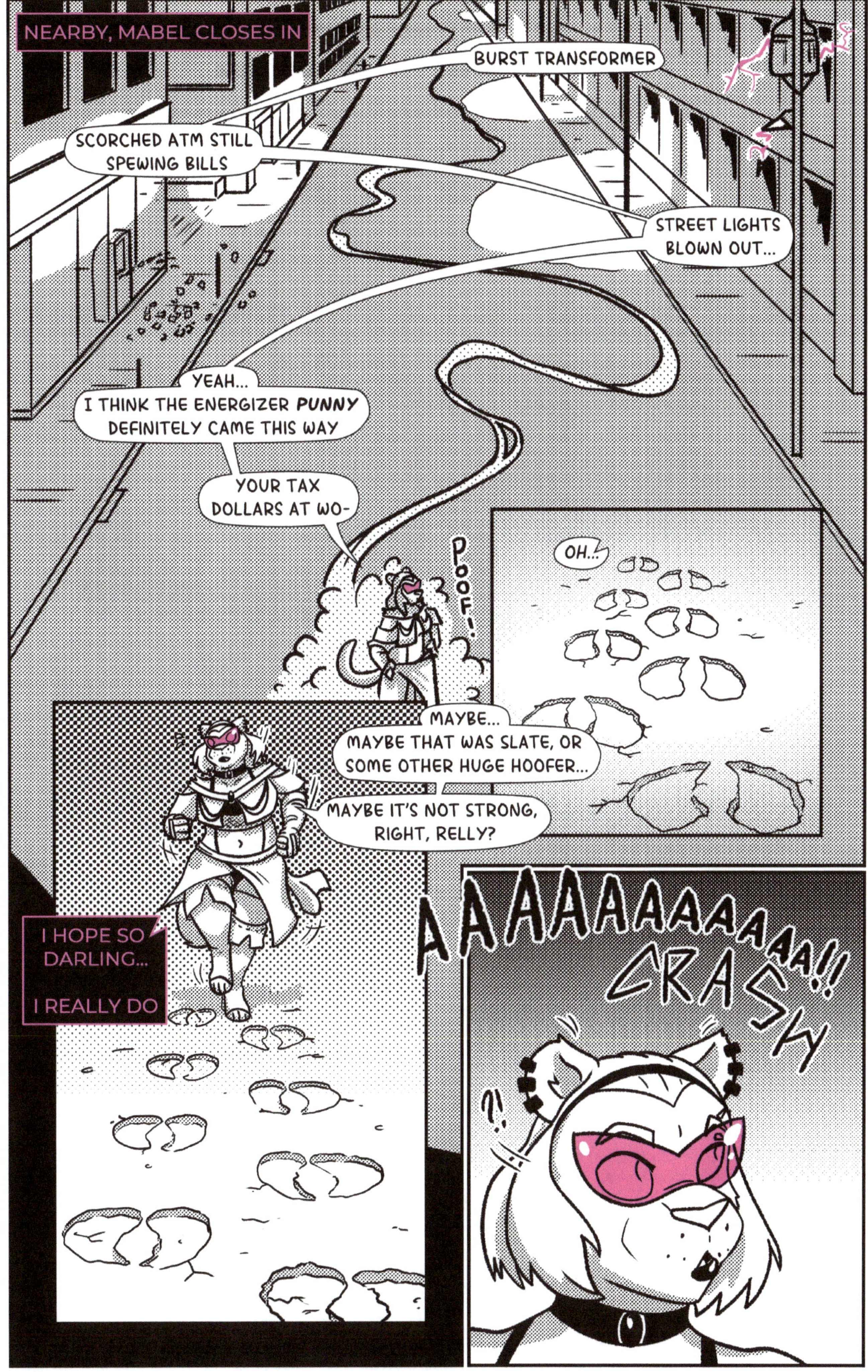

NEARBY, MABEL CLOSES IN
BURST TRANSFORMER
SCORCHED ATM STILL SPEWING BILLS
STREET LIGHTS BLOWN OUT...
YEAH... I THINK THE ENERGIZER PUNNY DEFINITELY CAME THIS WAY
YOUR TAX DOLLARS AT WO-
POOF!
OH...
MAYBE... MAYBE THAT WAS SLATE, OR SOME OTHER HUGE HOOFER...
MAYBE IT'S NOT STRONG, RIGHT, RELLY?
I HOPE SO DARLING...
I REALLY DO
AAAAAAAAAAA!!
CRASH

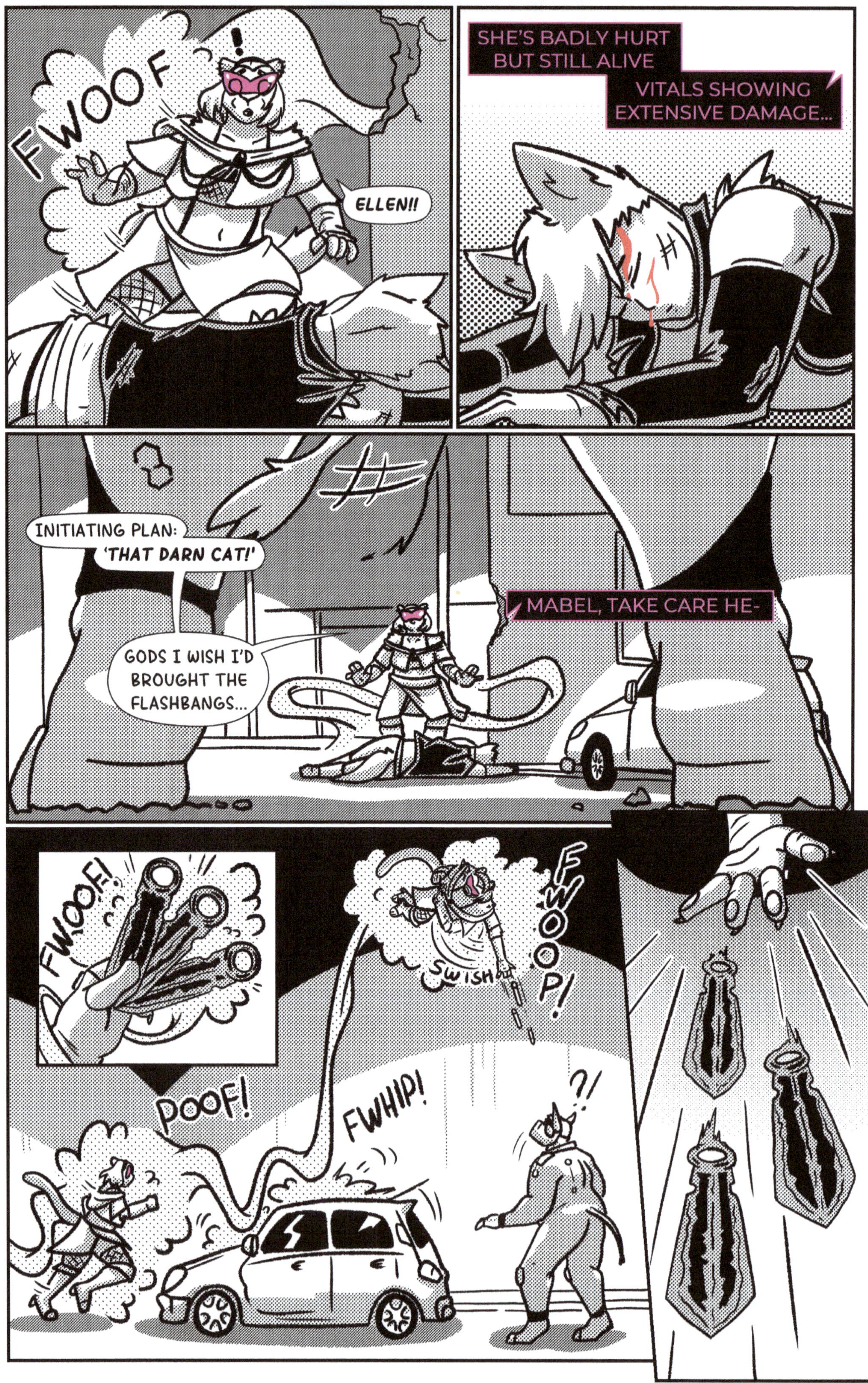
FWOOF
!
ELLEN!!
SHE'S BADLY HURT BUT STILL ALIVE
VITALS SHOWING EXTENSIVE DAMAGE...
INITIATING PLAN: 'THAT DARN CAT!'
GODS I WISH I'D BROUGHT THE FLASHBANGS...
MABEL, TAKE CARE HE-
FWOO!
POOF!
FWHIP!
SWISH
FWOOP!
?!

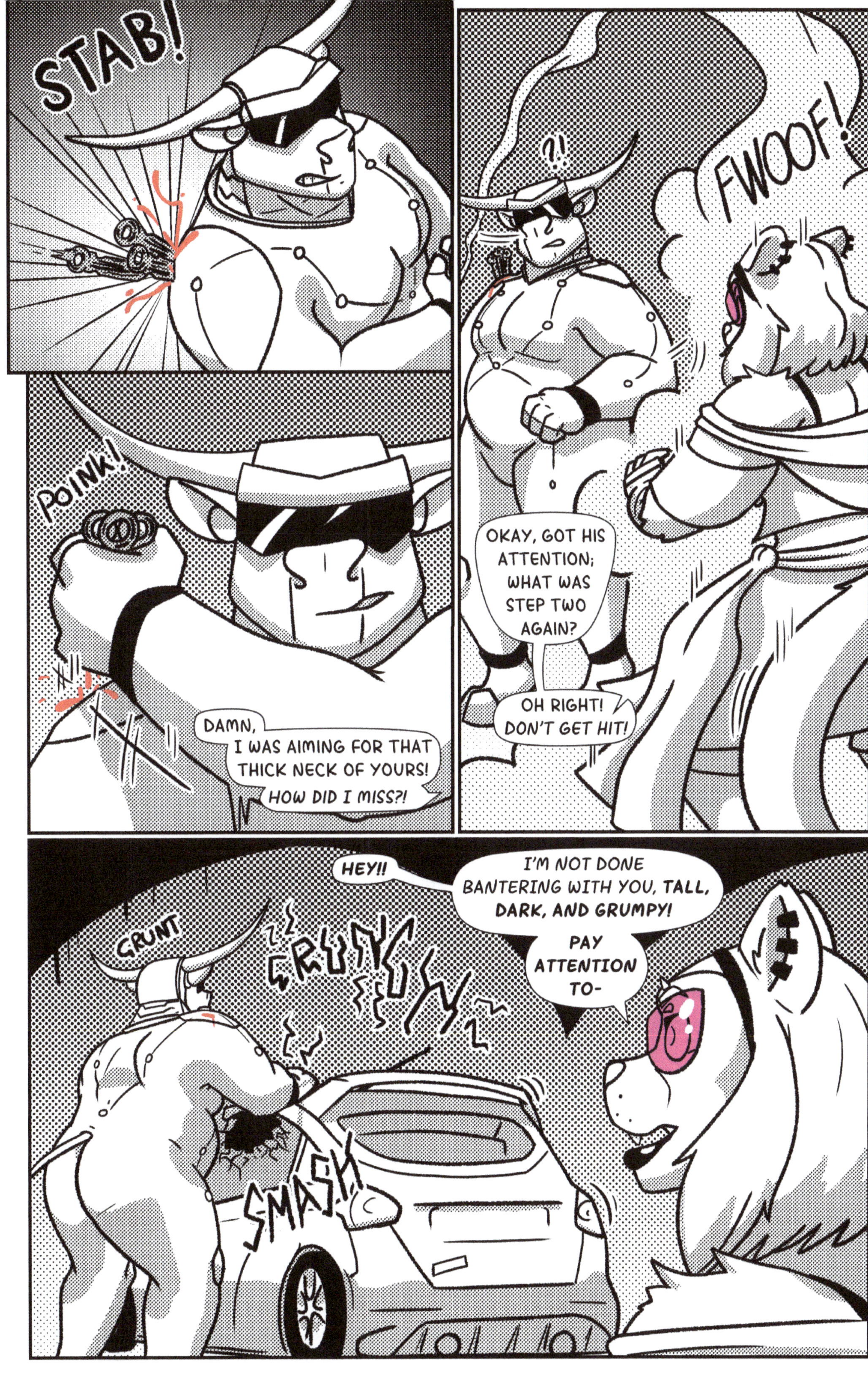

STAB!
FWOOF!
?!
POINK!
OKAY, GOT HIS ATTENTION; WHAT WAS STEP TWO AGAIN?
OH RIGHT! DON'T GET HIT!
DAMN, I WAS AIMING FOR THAT THICK NECK OF YOURS!
HOW DID I MISS?!
HEY!!
I'M NOT DONE BANTERING WITH YOU, TALL, DARK, AND GRUMPY!
PAY ATTENTION TO-
GRUNT
GRUNK
SMASH!

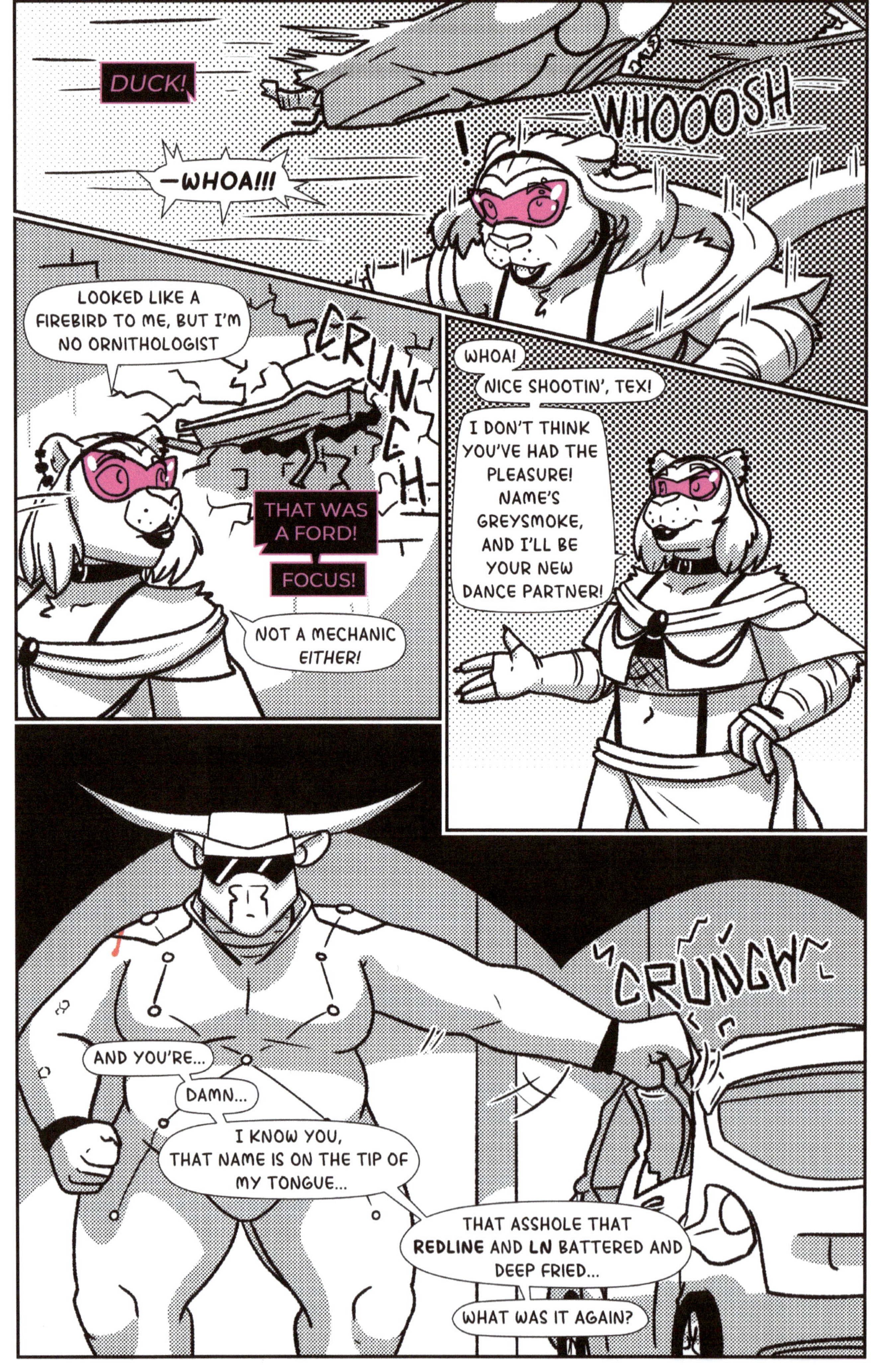
DUCK!
WHOOOSH
—WHOA!!!
!
LOOKED LIKE A FIREBIRD TO ME, BUT I'M NO ORNITHOLOGIST
CRUNCH
THAT WAS A FORD!
FOCUS!
NOT A MECHANIC EITHER!
WHOA! NICE SHOOTIN', TEX!
I DON'T THINK YOU'VE HAD THE PLEASURE! NAME'S GREYSMOKE, AND I'LL BE YOUR NEW DANCE PARTNER!
CRUNCH
AND YOU'RE...
DAMN...
I KNOW YOU, THAT NAME IS ON THE TIP OF MY TONGUE...
THAT ASSHOLE THAT REDLINE AND LN BATTERED AND DEEP FRIED...
WHAT WAS IT AGAIN?

IS YOUR RESPONSE ALWAYS JUST 'THROW CAR,' OR DO YOU HAVE ANY OTHER TRICKS, ASSHOLE?
NAME SHOULD HAVE BEEN PROPERTY DAMAGE!
OR INSURANCE CLAIM...
OR...
POOF
FWIP
THAT'S WHEN YOU SAY, 'I THROW PUNCHES, TOO, YOU STUPID SEXY CAT!' AND THEN I SAY...
POOF!
FWOOF!
SWING
'SEXY? SORRY, I DON'T GO FOR THE STRONG, SILENT TYPE!'
?
SEE THIS IS WHY HEROES AND VILLAINS DON'T GET ALONG! JUST NOT ENOUGH DIALOGUE...
HARD TO CHIT CHAT WHEN YOU'RE LICKING ALL THAT BOOT I SUPPOSE
YOU NEED TO NOT PROLONG THIS
IT NEEDS TO BE A RESCUE, NOT A FIGHT
POOF!
AGREED

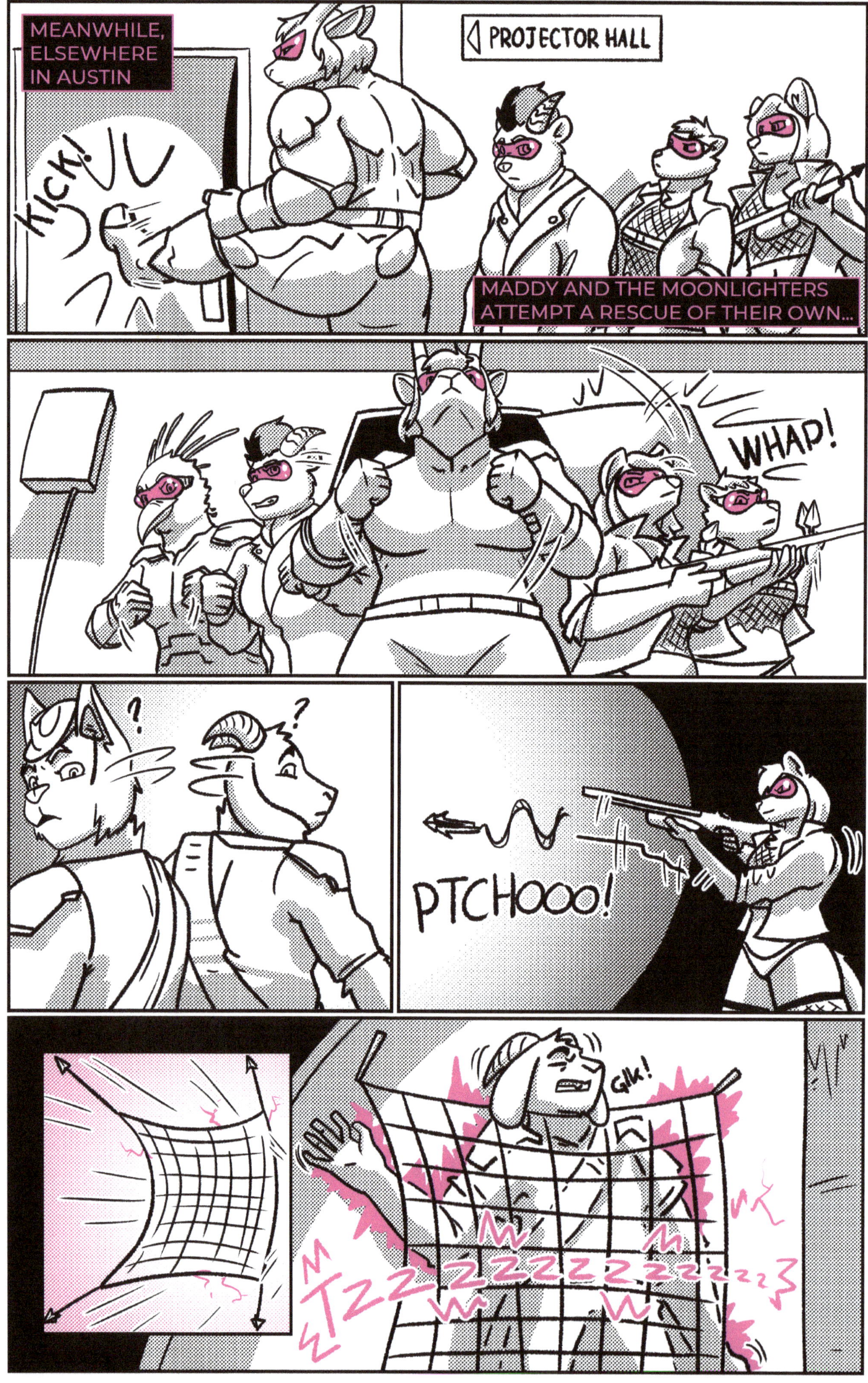

MEANWHILE, ELSEWHERE IN AUSTIN
KICK!
PROJECTOR HALL
MADDY AND THE MOONLIGHTERS ATTEMPT A RESCUE OF THEIR OWN...
WHAP!
?
?
PTCHOOO!
GUK!
ZZZZZZZZZZZZ

WE'VE GOT—
DUCK
T.P.A. 'TWILIGHT COWBOY'
T.P.A. COMMUNICATORS DETECTED! HIGHLIGHTING AS TARGET...
T.P.A. 'SCREAMING HALT'
T.P.A. 'BLACKWATER'

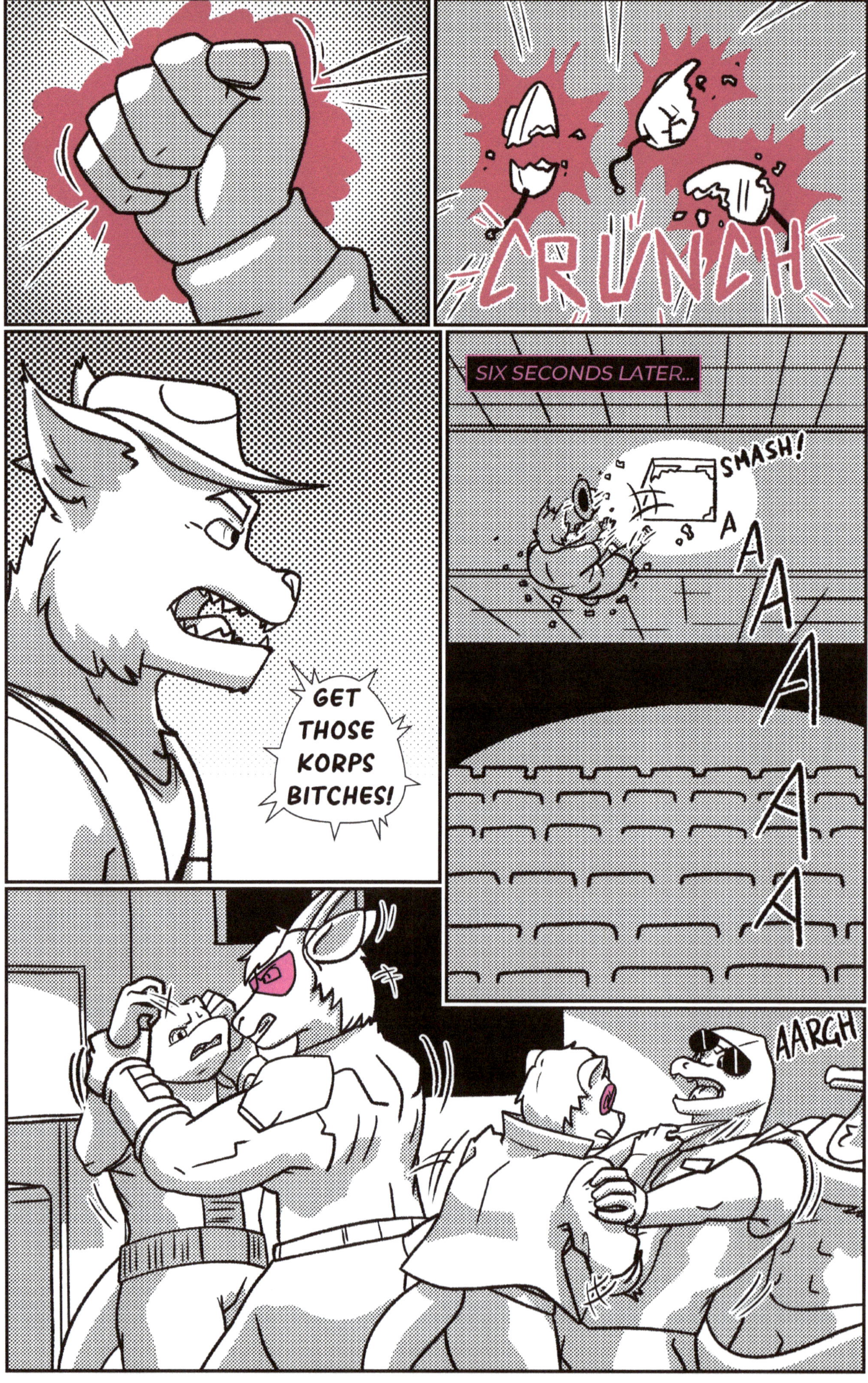

CRUNCH
SIX SECONDS LATER...
SMASH!
AAAAA
GET THOSE KORPS BITCHES!
AARGH

!
HEY, MARSHLIGHT! REMEMBER ME...?
WAIT, WHO—
?!!
WHACK!!
CRUNCH!
TOSS!
FWIP!
AAAH!!
PATHETIC

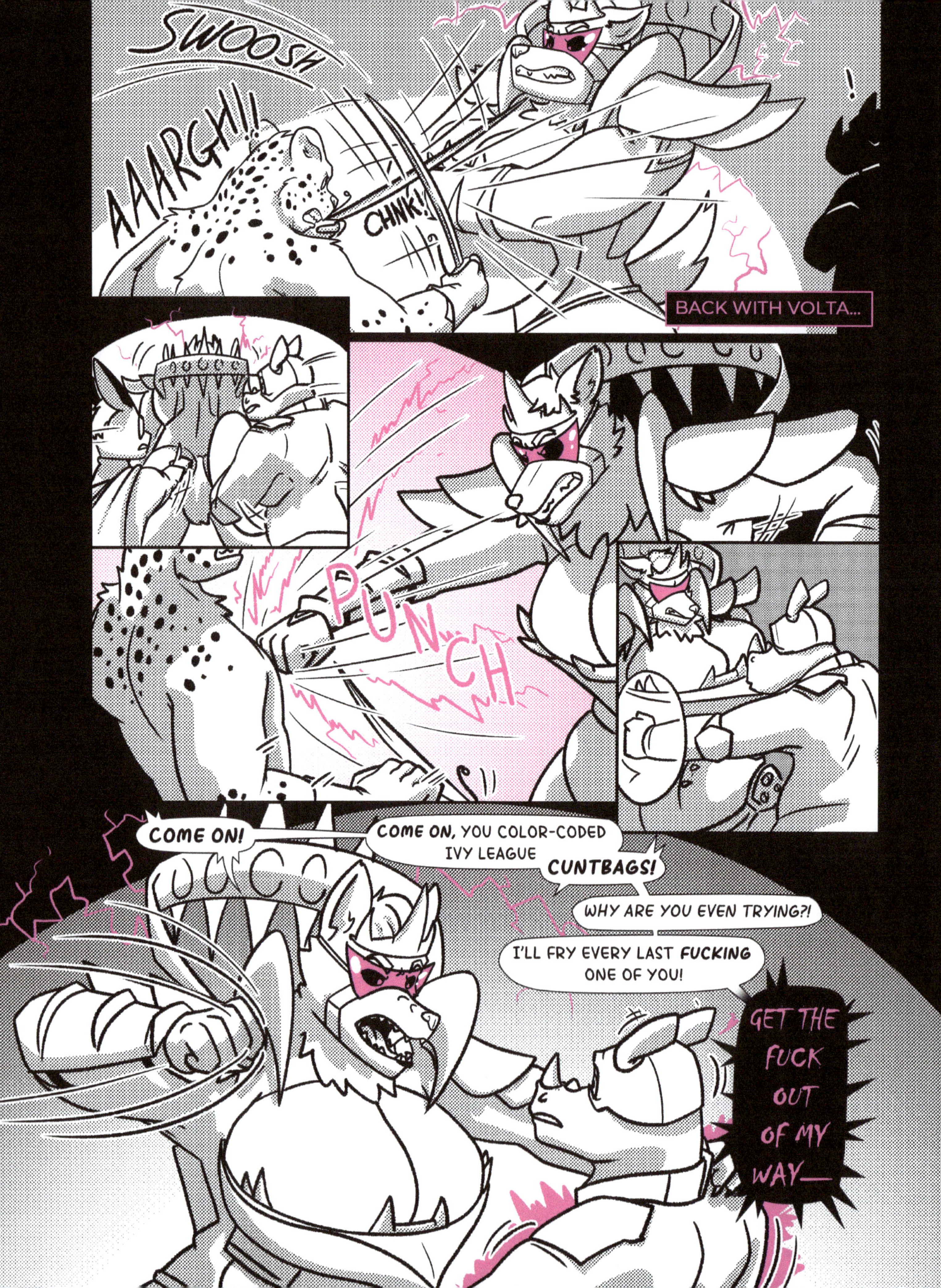

SWOOSH
AAARGH!!!
CHNK!
BACK WITH VOLTA...
PUNCH
COME ON!
COME ON, YOU COLOR-CODED IVY LEAGUE CUNTBAGS!
WHY ARE YOU EVEN TRYING?!
I'LL FRY EVERY LAST FUCKING ONE OF YOU!
GET THE FUCK OUT OF MY WAY—

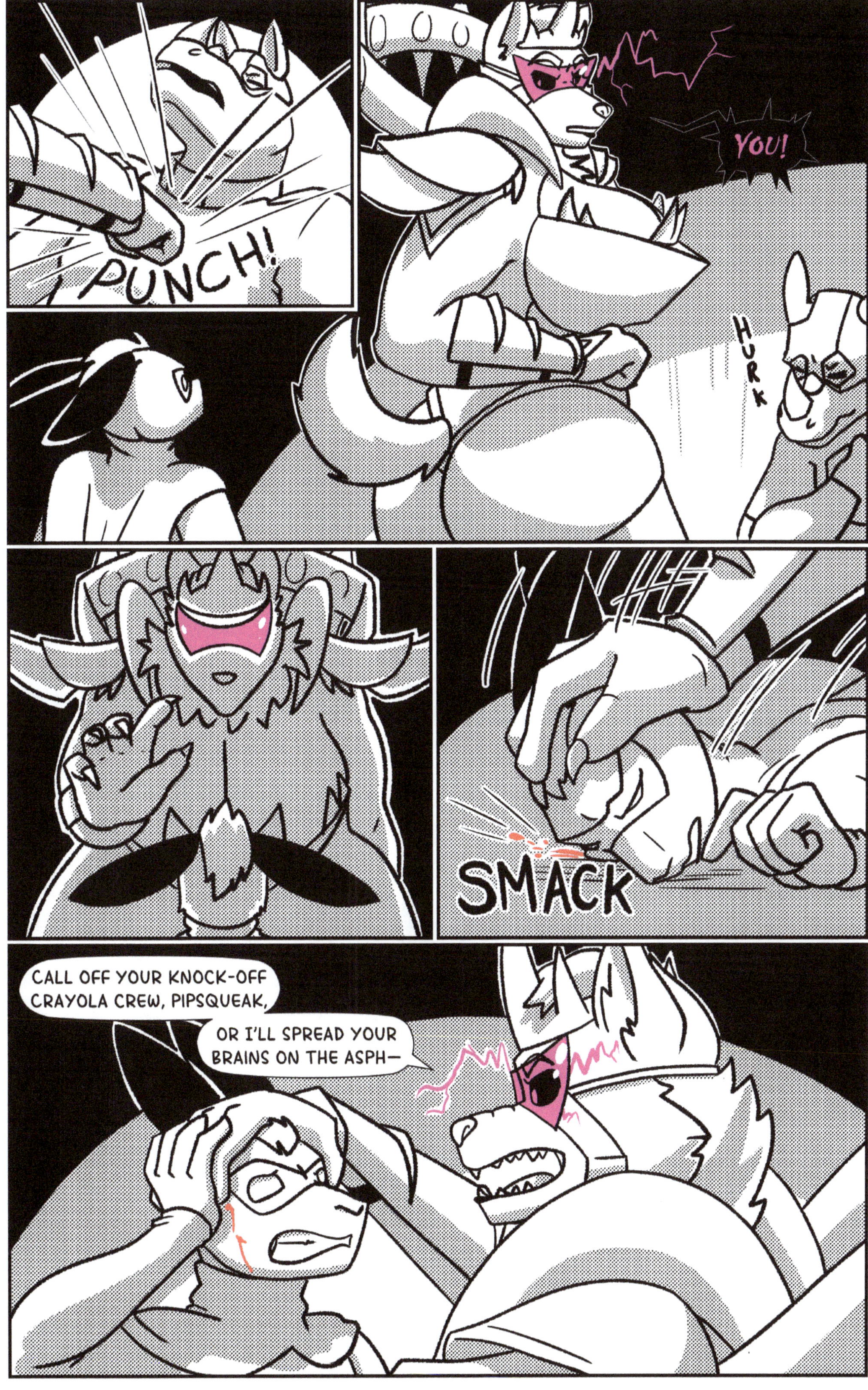
PUNCH!
YOU!
HURK
SMACK
CALL OFF YOUR KNOCK-OFF CRAYOLA CREW, PIPSQUEAK,
OR I'LL SPREAD YOUR BRAINS ON THE ASPH—

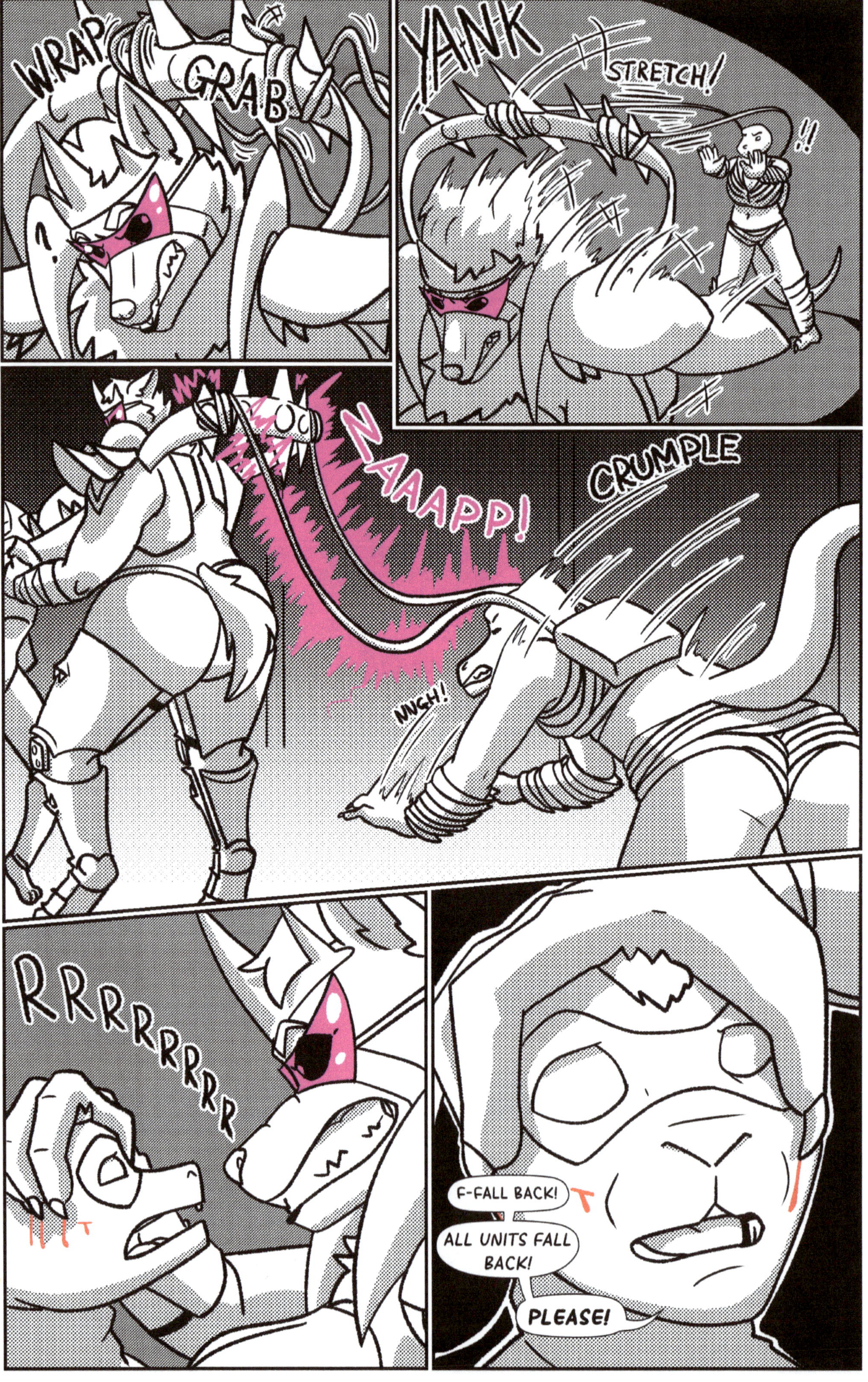

WRAP
GRAB
YANK
STRETCH!
NAAAPP!
MNGH!
CRUMPLE
RRRRRRRR
F-FALL BACK!
ALL UNITS FALL BACK!
PLEASE!

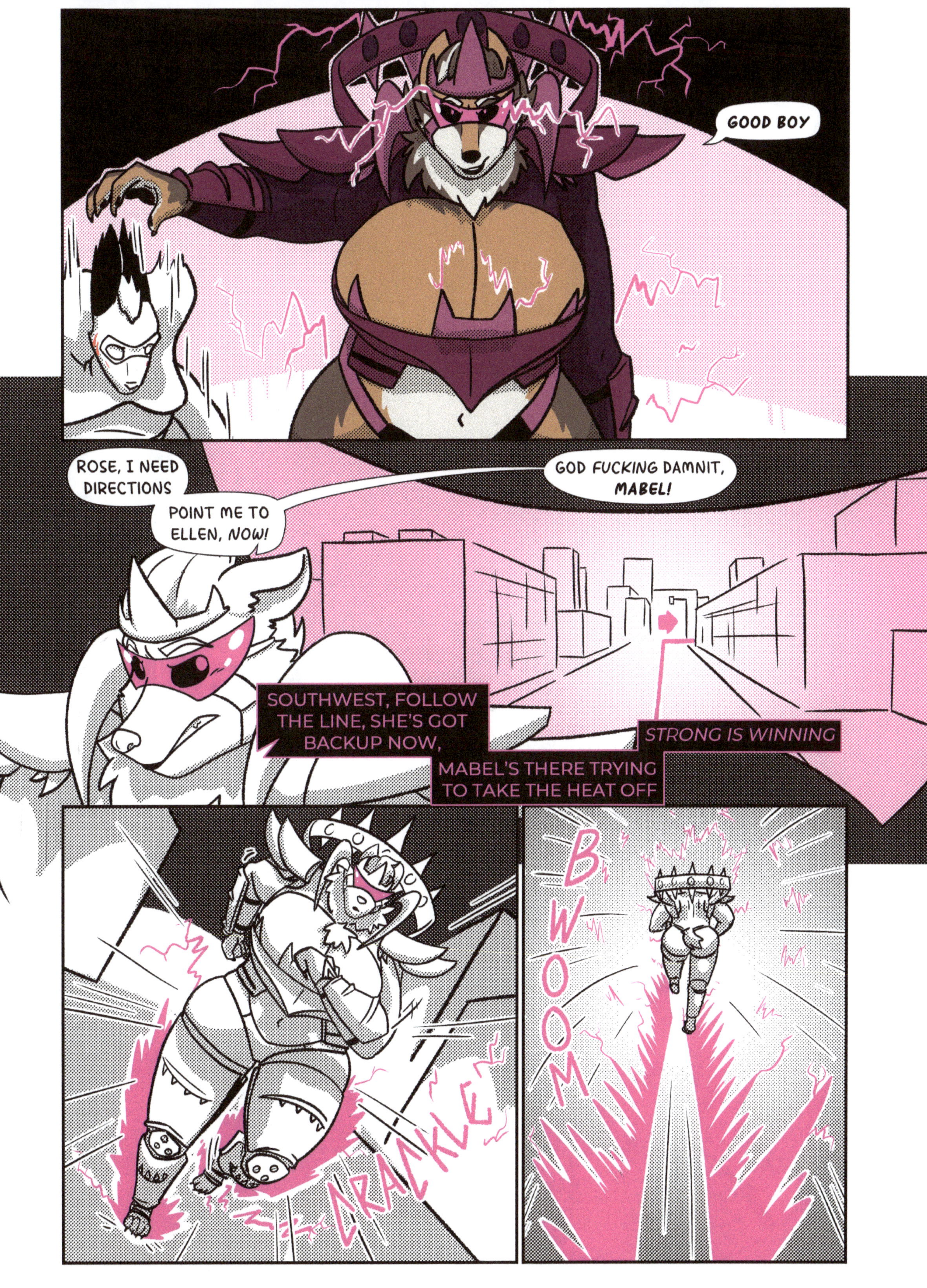

GOOD BOY
ROSE, I NEED DIRECTIONS
POINT ME TO ELLEN, NOW!
GOD FUCKING DAMNIT, MABEL!
SOUTHWEST, FOLLOW THE LINE, SHE'S GOT BACKUP NOW,
MABEL'S THERE TRYING TO TAKE THE HEAT OFF
STRONG IS WINNING
CRACKLE
BWOOM

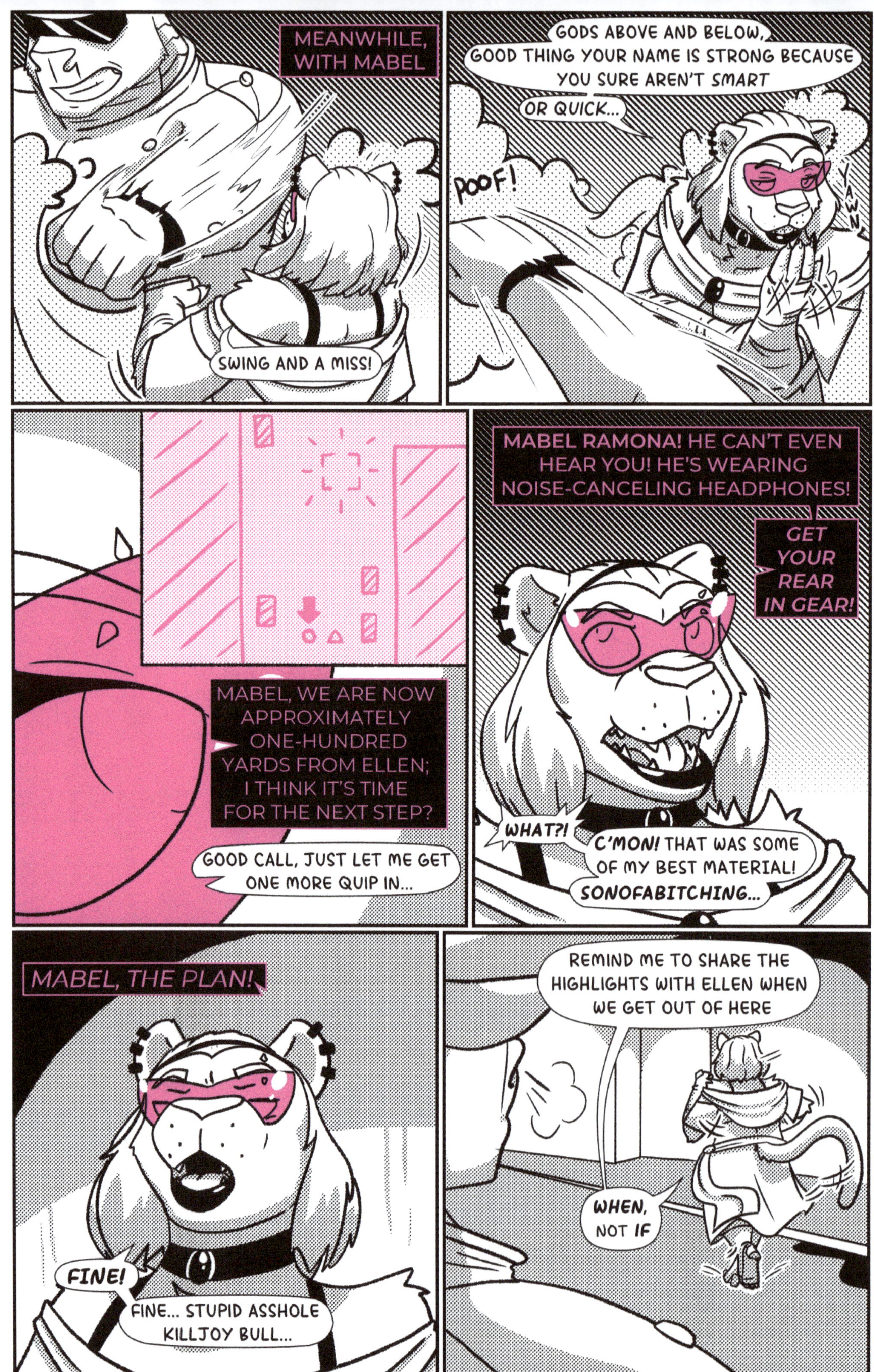

MEANWHILE, WITH MABEL
SWING AND A MISS!
GODS ABOVE AND BELOW, GOOD THING YOUR NAME IS STRONG BECAUSE YOU SURE AREN'T SMART OR QUICK...
POOF!
MABEL, WE ARE NOW APPROXIMATELY ONE-HUNDRED YARDS FROM ELLEN; I THINK IT'S TIME FOR THE NEXT STEP?
GOOD CALL, JUST LET ME GET ONE MORE QUIP IN...
MABEL RAMONA! HE CAN'T EVEN HEAR YOU! HE'S WEARING NOISE-CANCELING HEADPHONES!
GET YOUR REAR IN GEAR!
WHAT?!
C'MON! THAT WAS SOME OF MY BEST MATERIAL!
SONOFABITCHING...
MABEL, THE PLAN!
FINE!
FINE... STUPID ASSHOLE KILLJOY BULL...
REMIND ME TO SHARE THE HIGHLIGHTS WITH ELLEN WHEN WE GET OUT OF HERE
WHEN, NOT IF

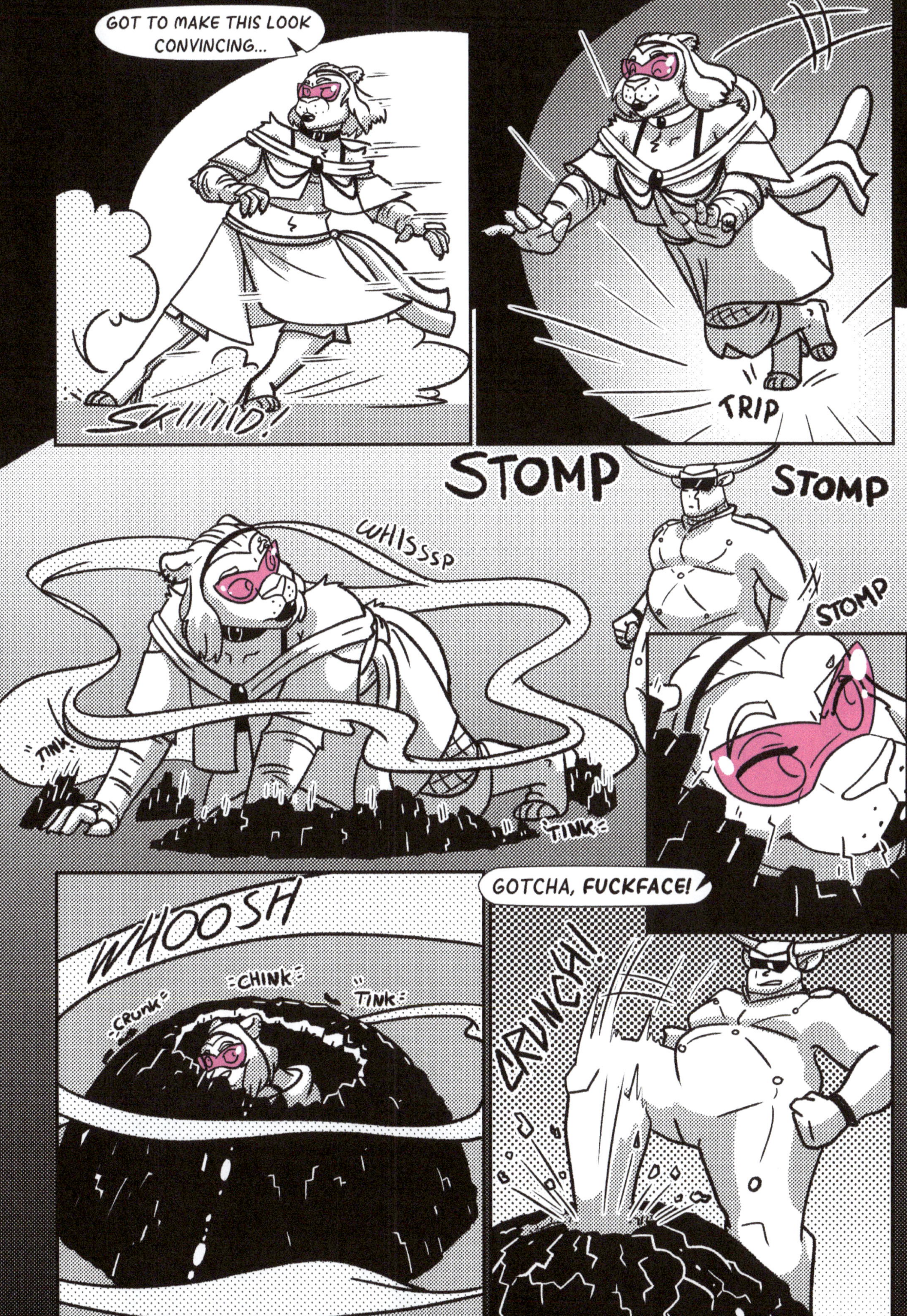

GOT TO MAKE THIS LOOK CONVINCING...
SKIIIID!
TRIP
STOMP
STOMP
STOMP
WHISsssp
TINK
TINK
WHOOSH
CRUNK
CHINK
TINK
GOTCHA, FUCKFACE!
CRUNCH!!

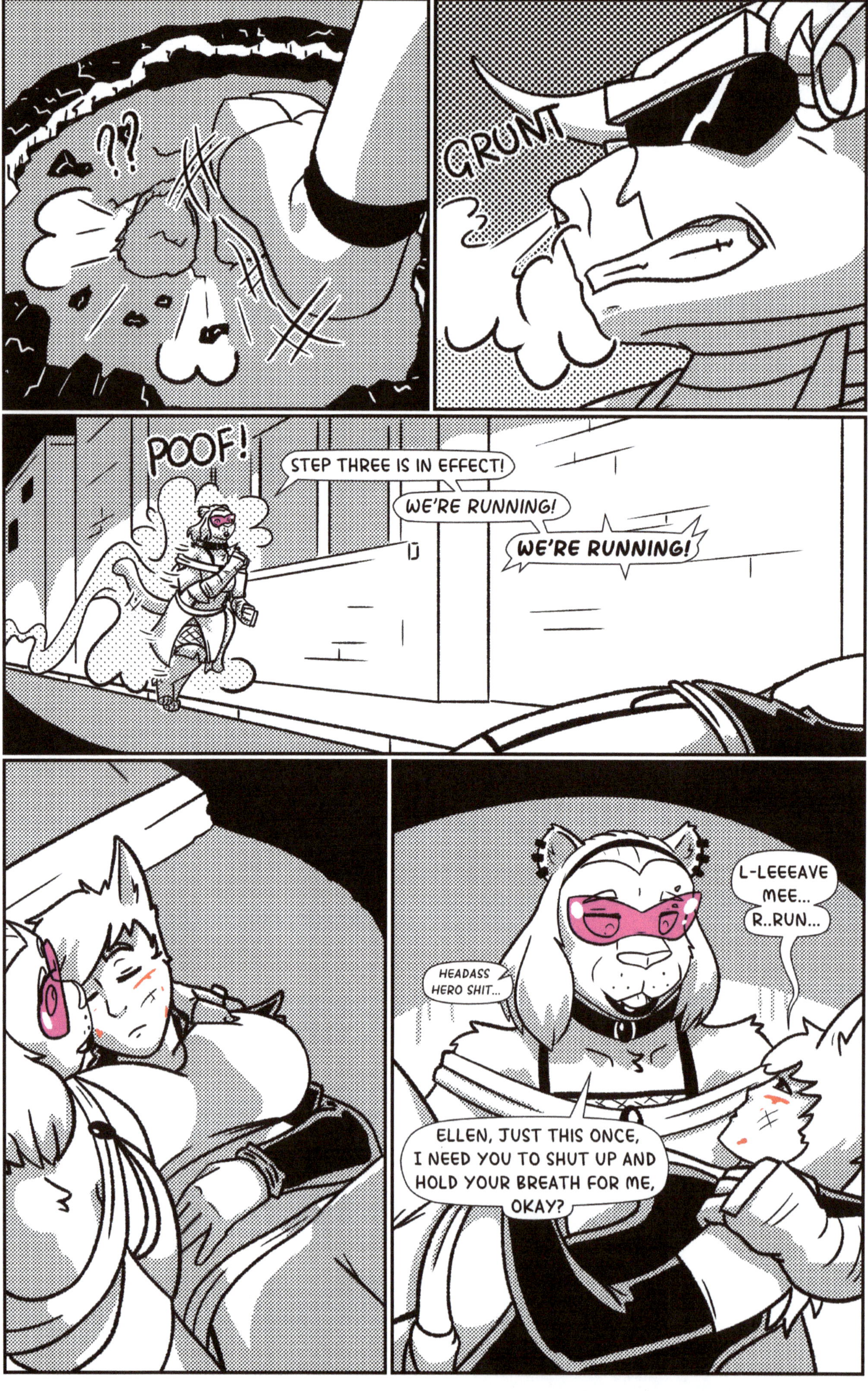
??
GRUNT
POOF!
STEP THREE IS IN EFFECT!
WE'RE RUNNING!
WE'RE RUNNING!
L-LEEEAVE MEE... R..RUN...
HEADASS HERO SHIT...
ELLEN, JUST THIS ONCE, I NEED YOU TO SHUT UP AND HOLD YOUR BREATH FOR ME, OKAY?

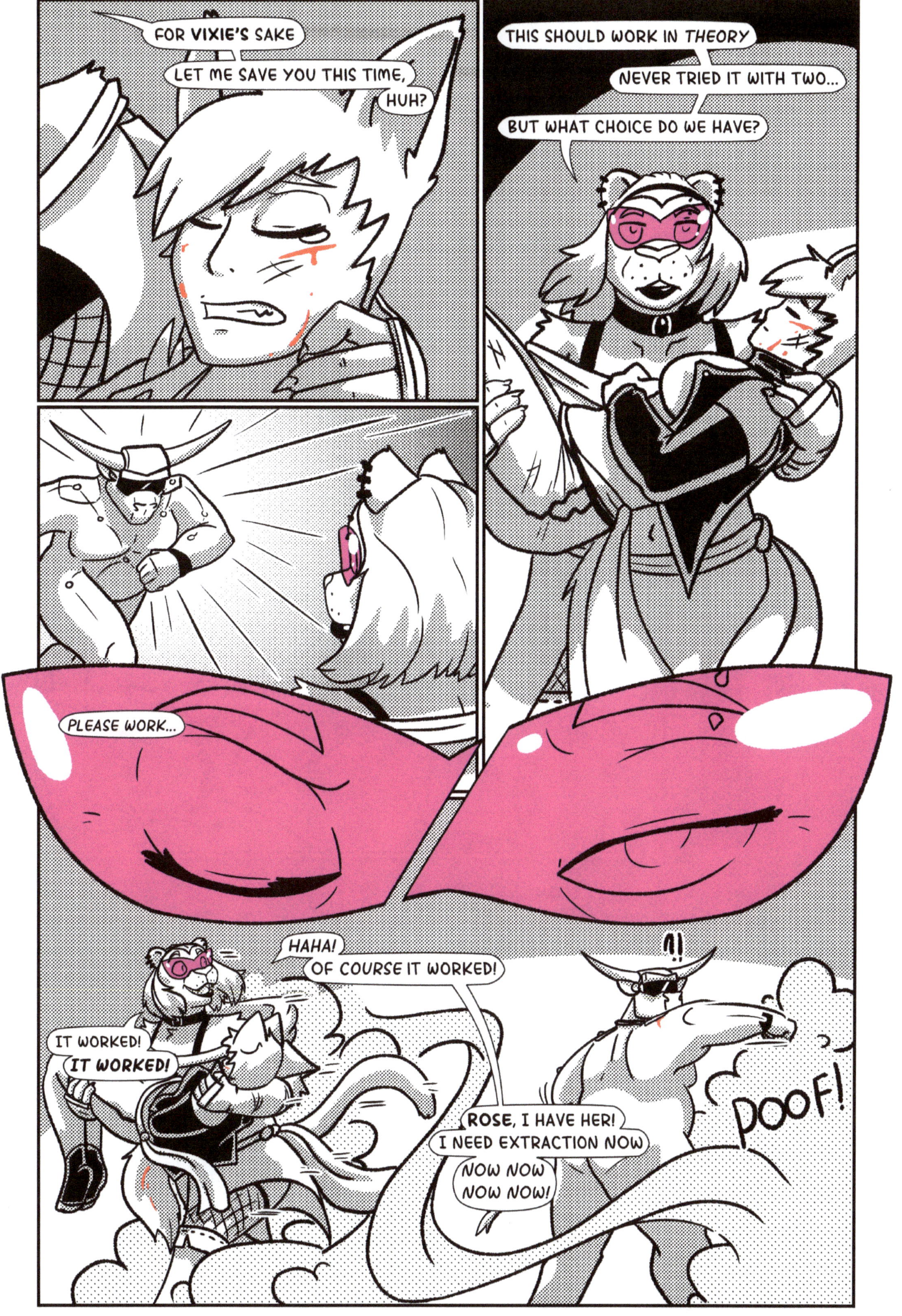

FOR VIXIE'S SAKE
LET ME SAVE YOU THIS TIME, HUH?
THIS SHOULD WORK IN THEORY
NEVER TRIED IT WITH TWO...
BUT WHAT CHOICE DO WE HAVE?
PLEASE WORK...
HAHA!
OF COURSE IT WORKED!
IT WORKED!
IT WORKED!
ROSE, I HAVE HER!
I NEED EXTRACTION NOW
NOW NOW NOW NOW!
POOF!

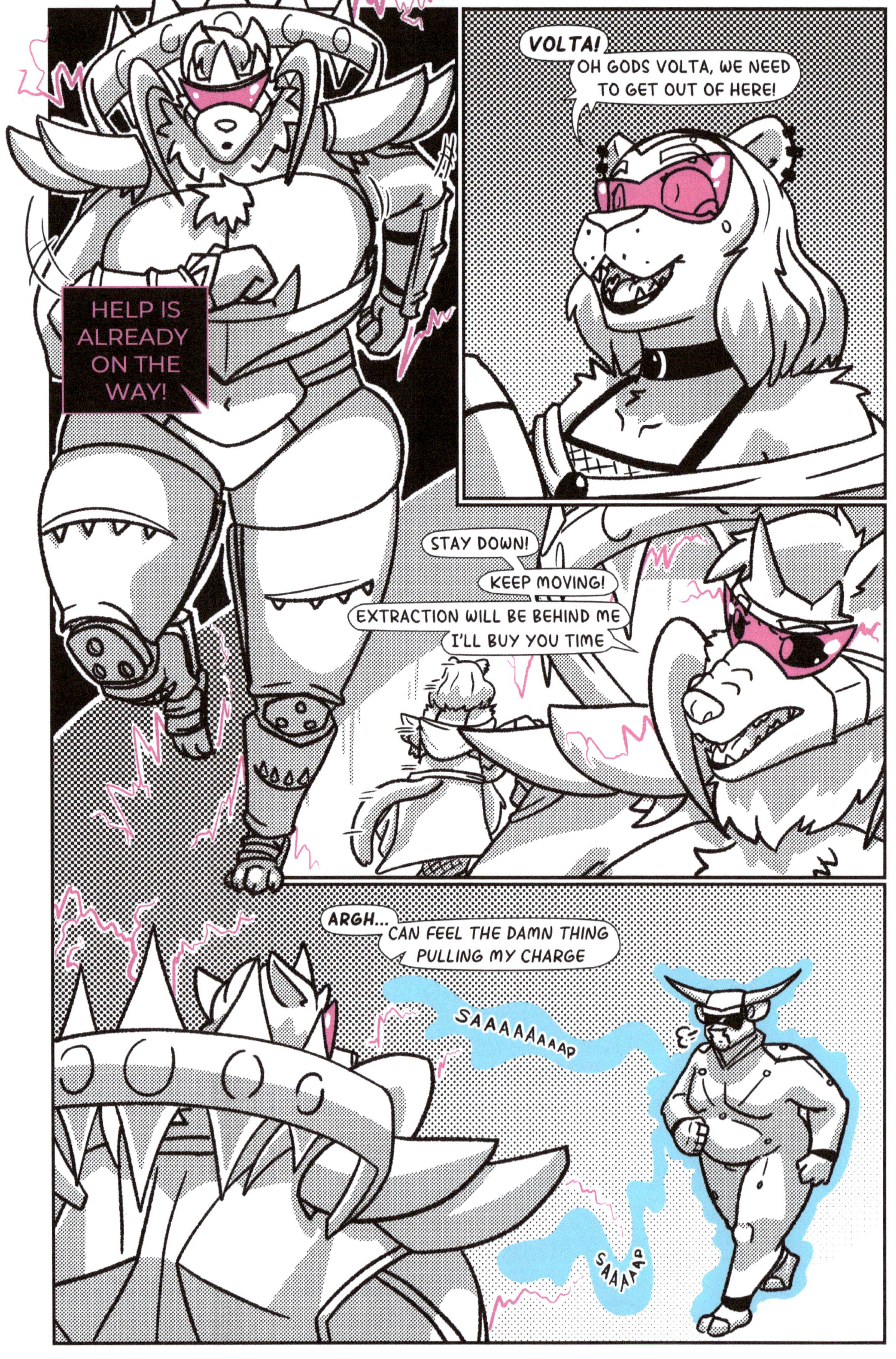
HELP IS ALREADY ON THE WAY!
VOLTA!
OH GODS VOLTA, WE NEED TO GET OUT OF HERE!
STAY DOWN!
KEEP MOVING!
EXTRACTION WILL BE BEHIND ME I'LL BUY YOU TIME
ARGH...
CAN FEEL THE DAMN THING PULLING MY CHARGE
SAAAAAAAAP
SAAAAP

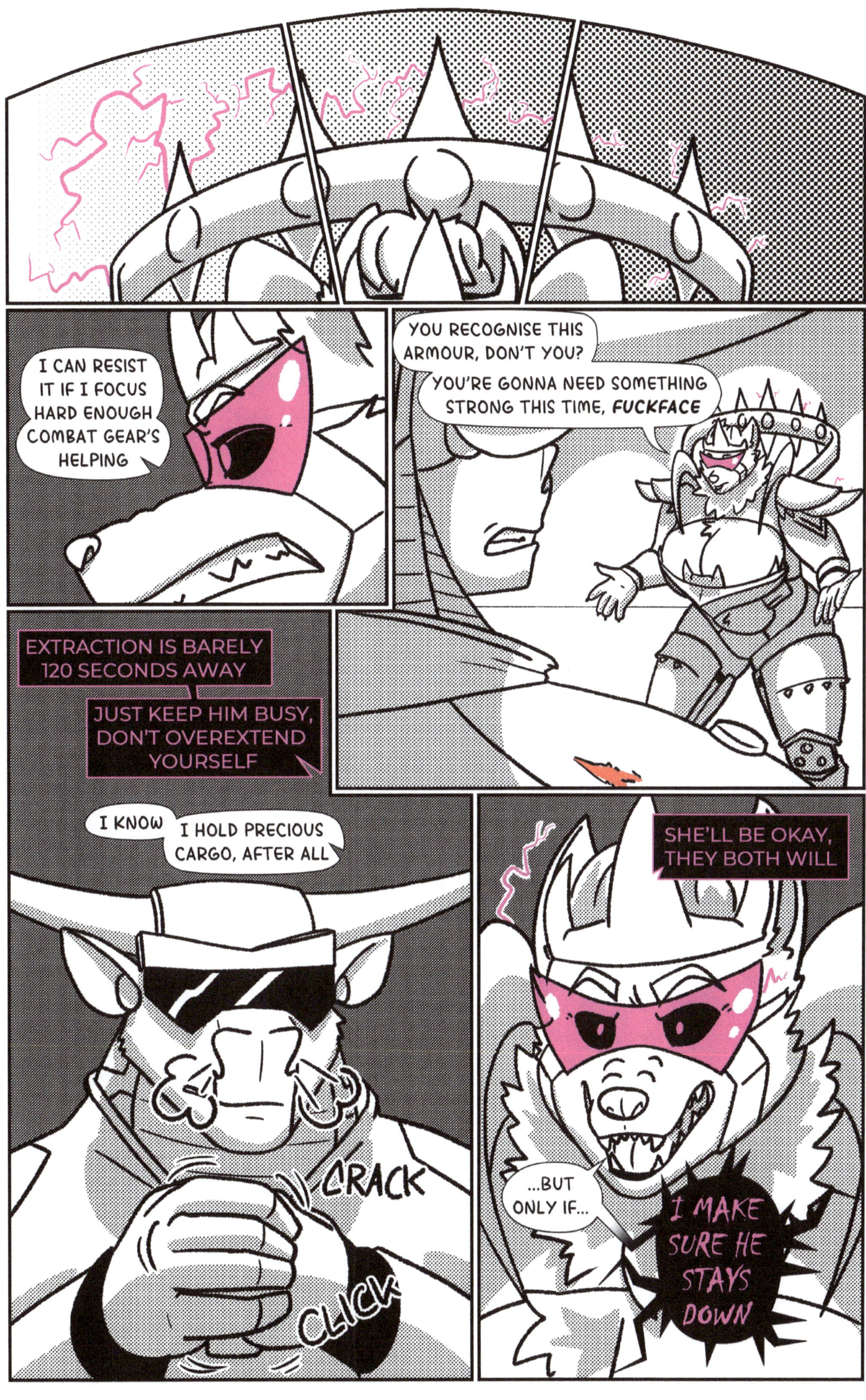
I CAN RESIST IT IF I FOCUS HARD ENOUGH COMBAT GEAR'S HELPING
YOU RECOGNISE THIS ARMOUR, DON'T YOU?
YOU'RE GONNA NEED SOMETHING STRONG THIS TIME, FUCKFACE
EXTRACTION IS BARELY 120 SECONDS AWAY
JUST KEEP HIM BUSY, DON'T OVEREXTEND YOURSELF
I KNOW
I HOLD PRECIOUS CARGO, AFTER ALL
CRACK
CLICK
SHE'LL BE OKAY, THEY BOTH WILL
...BUT ONLY IF...
I MAKE SURE HE STAYS DOWN

PUNCH
BLOCK
SMACK
ERK!
SLAM!!
PTOO
REACH
GRAB

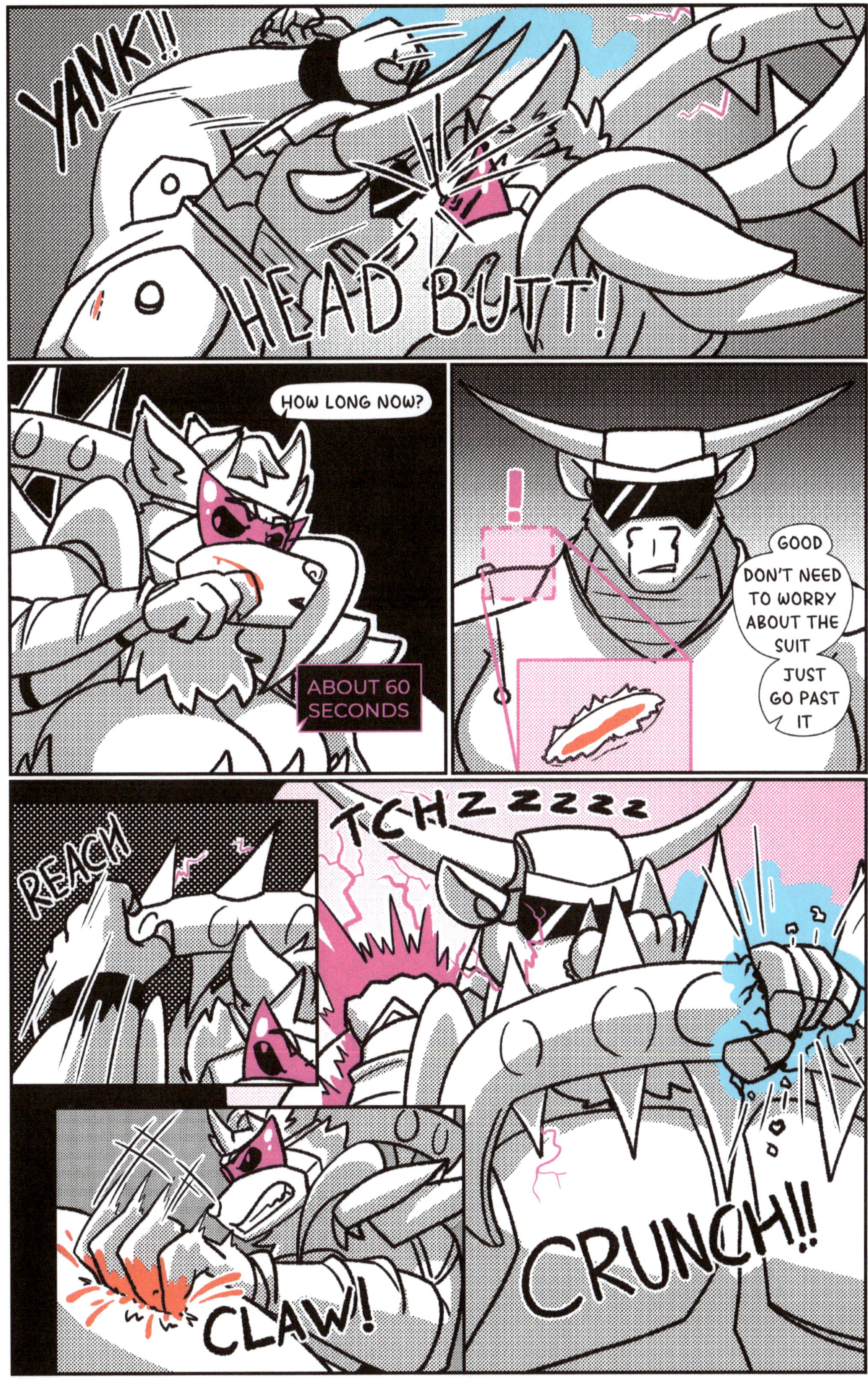

YANK!!
HEAD BUTT!
HOW LONG NOW?
ABOUT 60 SECONDS
GOOD
DON'T NEED TO WORRY ABOUT THE SUIT
JUST GO PAST IT
REACH!
TCHZZZZZ
CLAW!
CRUNCH!!

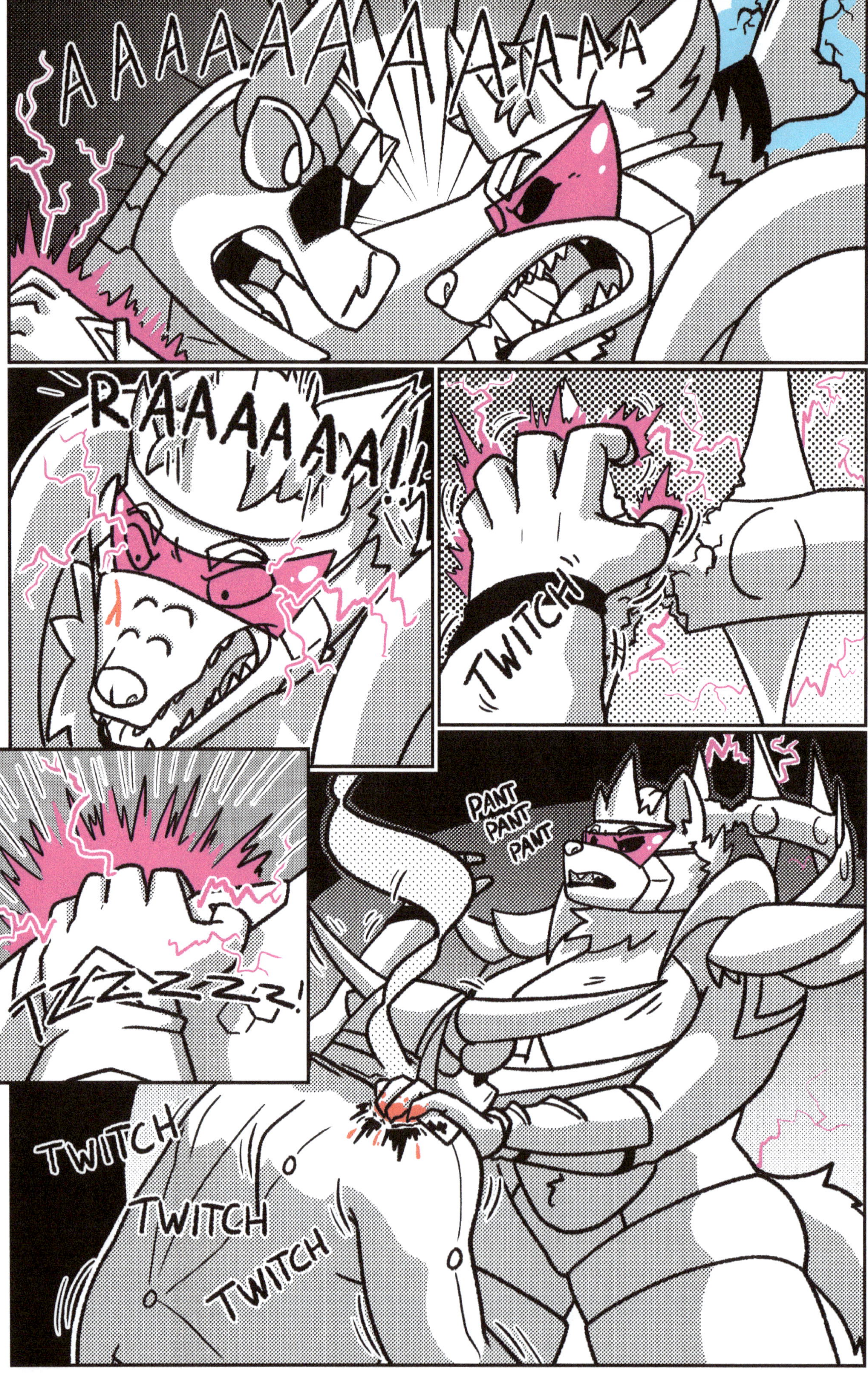

AAAAAAAA AAAA
RAAAAAAA!
TWITCH
TZZZZZZZ!
PANT PANT PANT
TWITCH
TWITCH
TWITCH

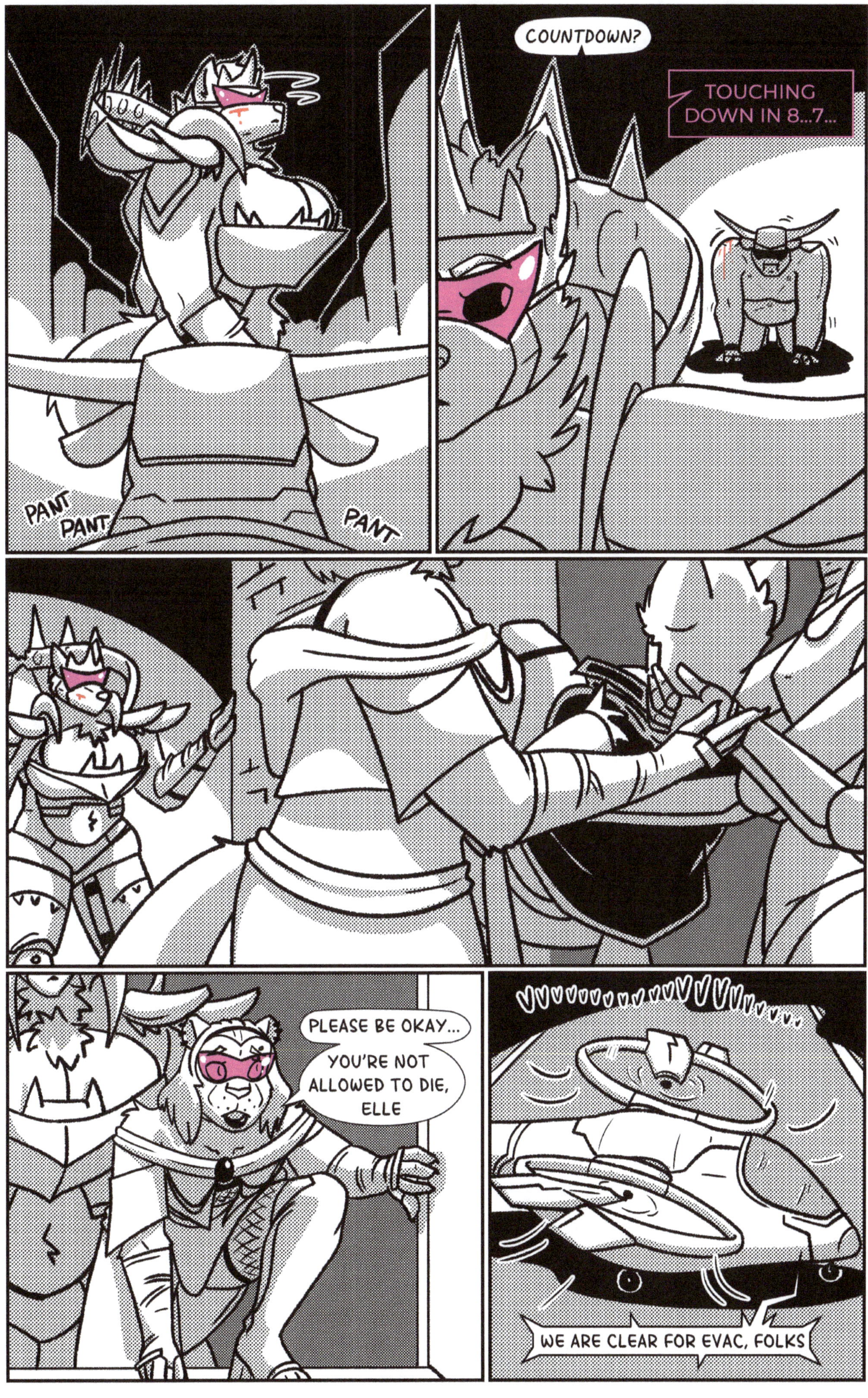

PANT PANT
PANT
COUNTDOWN?
TOUCHING DOWN IN 8...7...
PLEASE BE OKAY...
YOU'RE NOT ALLOWED TO DIE, ELLE
WE ARE CLEAR FOR EVAC, FOLKS

CAN WE GET HER CONSCIOUS?
We'll see. While she can try to heal herself with her powers, she would likely be in too much pain to deliver a joke worth telling. We will do what we can for now until we can get her to that point.
RUB
RUB
MABES, YOU NEED TO CALM DOWN, SHE'S IN THE BEST POSSIBLE PAWS RIGHT NOW
I SHOULD HAVE GOTTEN THERE SOONER
I SHOULD HAVE KNOWN AS SOON AS SHE WENT DARK THAT SOMETHING WAS WRONG...
YOU SHOULDN'T HAVE EVEN BEEN THERE AT ALL

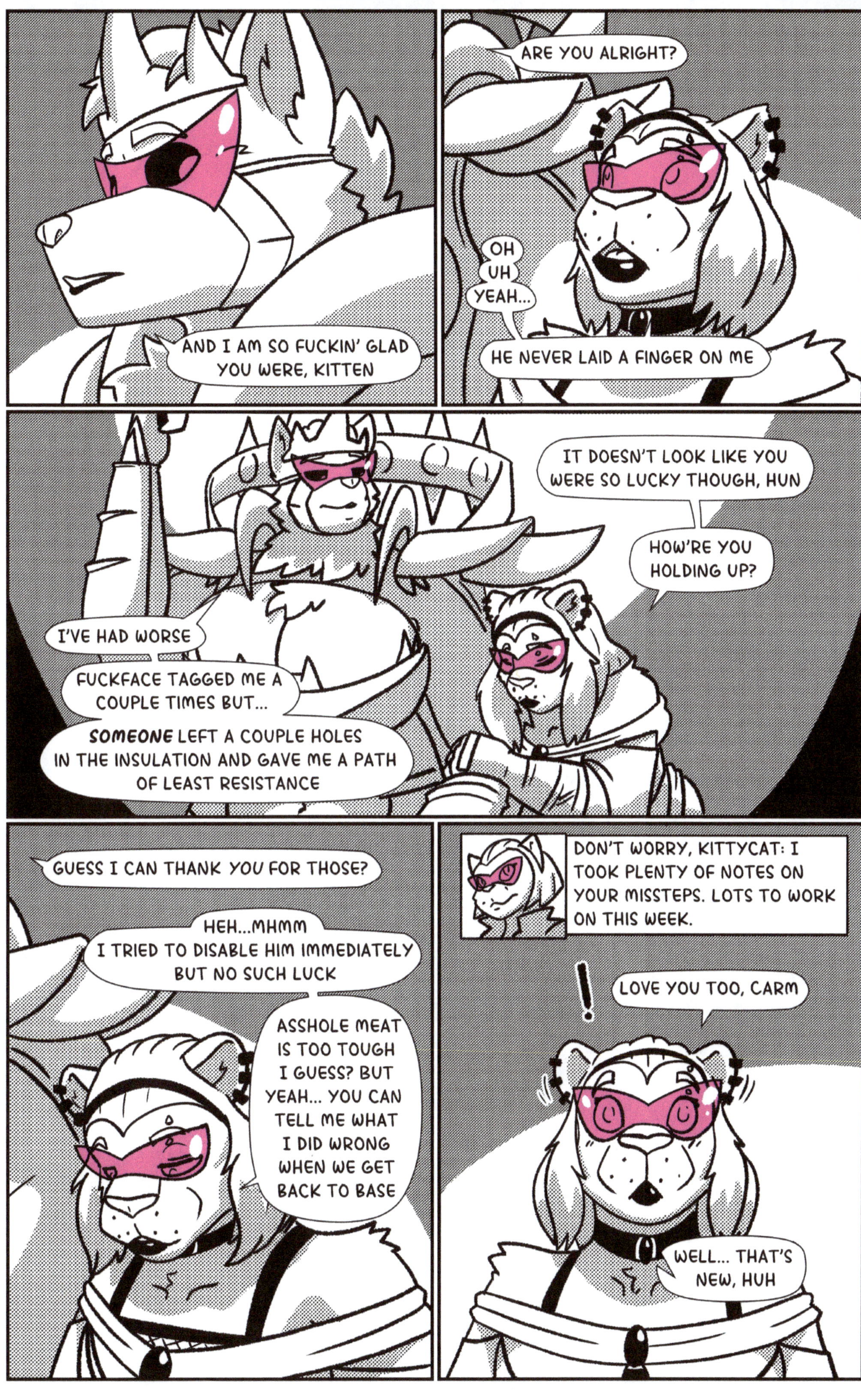

AND I AM SO FUCKIN' GLAD YOU WERE, KITTEN
ARE YOU ALRIGHT?
OH UH) YEAH...
HE NEVER LAID A FINGER ON ME
IT DOESN'T LOOK LIKE YOU WERE SO LUCKY THOUGH, HUN
HOW'RE YOU HOLDING UP?
I'VE HAD WORSE
FUCKFACE TAGGED ME A COUPLE TIMES BUT...
SOMEONE LEFT A COUPLE HOLES IN THE INSULATION AND GAVE ME A PATH OF LEAST RESISTANCE
GUESS I CAN THANK YOU FOR THOSE?
HEH...MHMM
I TRIED TO DISABLE HIM IMMEDIATELY BUT NO SUCH LUCK
ASSHOLE MEAT IS TOO TOUGH I GUESS? BUT YEAH... YOU CAN TELL ME WHAT I DID WRONG WHEN WE GET BACK TO BASE
DON'T WORRY, KITTYCAT: I TOOK PLENTY OF NOTES ON YOUR MISSTEPS. LOTS TO WORK ON THIS WEEK.
LOVE YOU TOO, CARM
WELL... THAT'S NEW, HUH

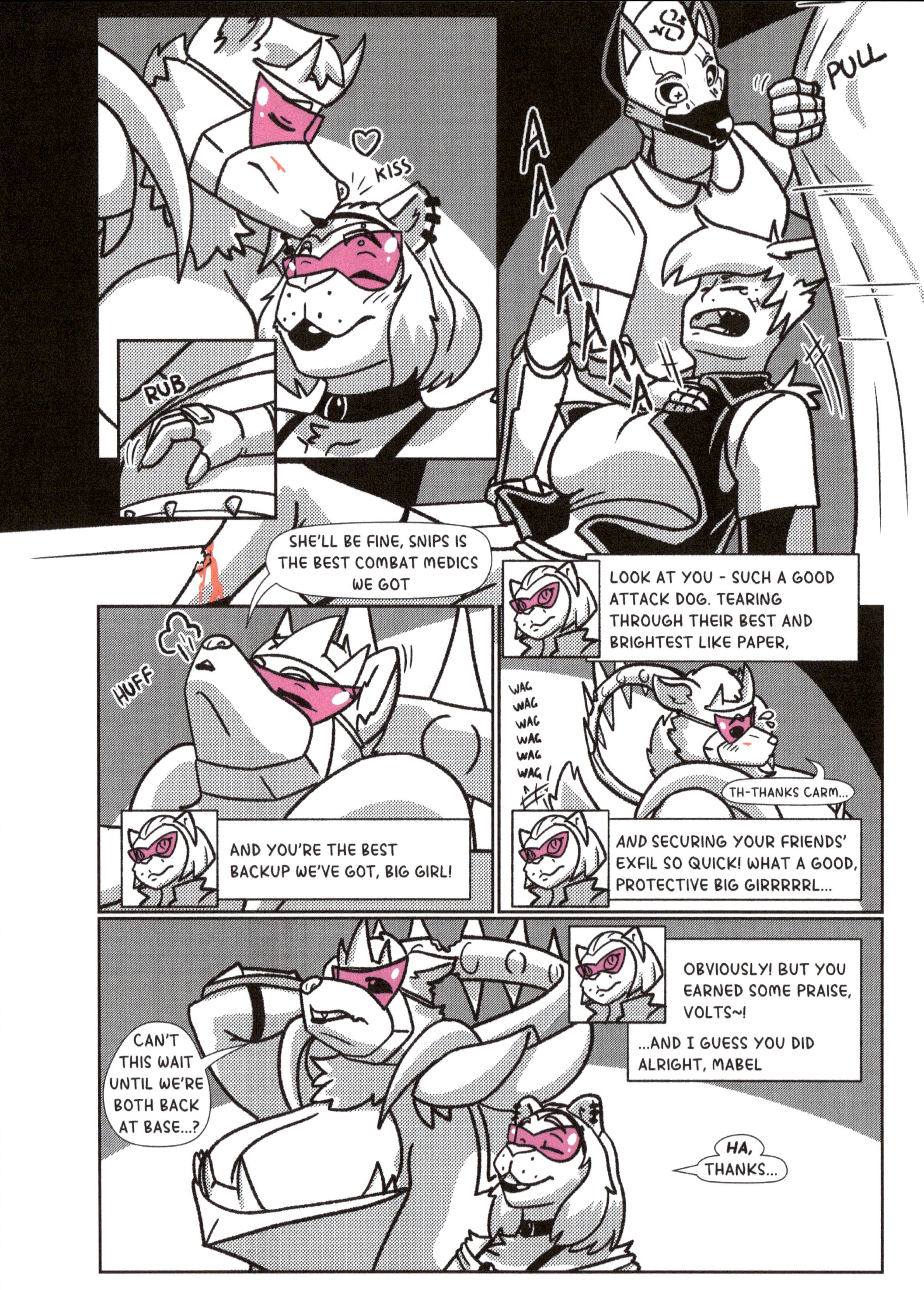

KISS
PULL
A A A A A A A A A
RUB
SHE'LL BE FINE, SNIPS IS THE BEST COMBAT MEDICS WE GOT
LOOK AT YOU - SUCH A GOOD ATTACK DOG. TEARING THROUGH THEIR BEST AND BRIGHTEST LIKE PAPER,
HUFF
WAG WAG WAG WAG WAG WAG
TH-THANKS CARM...
AND YOU'RE THE BEST BACKUP WE'VE GOT, BIG GIRL!
AND SECURING YOUR FRIENDS' EXFIL SO QUICK! WHAT A GOOD, PROTECTIVE BIG GIRRRRRL...
OBVIOUSLY! BUT YOU EARNED SOME PRAISE, VOLTS~!
...AND I GUESS YOU DID ALRIGHT, MABEL
CAN'T THIS WAIT UNTIL WE'RE BOTH BACK AT BASE...?
HA, THANKS...

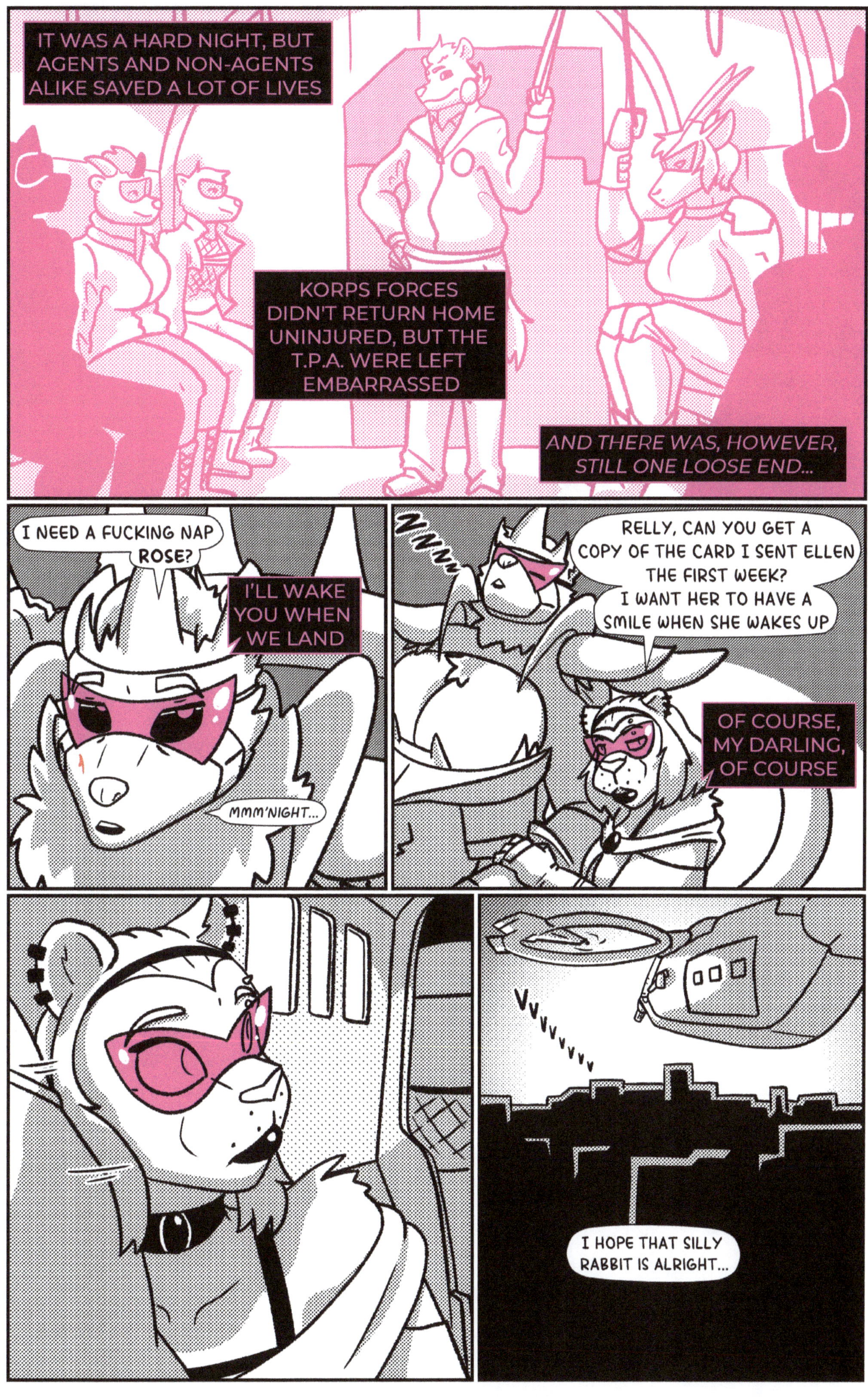

IT WAS A HARD NIGHT, BUT AGENTS AND NON-AGENTS ALIKE SAVED A LOT OF LIVES
KORPS FORCES DIDN'T RETURN HOME UNINJURED, BUT THE T.P.A. WERE LEFT EMBARRASSED
AND THERE WAS, HOWEVER, STILL ONE LOOSE END...
I NEED A FUCKING NAP ROSE?
I'LL WAKE YOU WHEN WE LAND
MMM'NIGHT...
RELLY, CAN YOU GET A COPY OF THE CARD I SENT ELLEN THE FIRST WEEK? I WANT HER TO HAVE A SMILE WHEN SHE WAKES UP
OF COURSE, MY DARLING, OF COURSE
VVVVVVVV
I HOPE THAT SILLY RABBIT IS ALRIGHT...

THESE STORIES CONTINUE...

WHO ARE THE KORPS?

8

ON A PARALLEL EARTH, THE ARRIVAL OF A TRAVELER FROM BEYOND THE STARS CHANGED THE FACE OF HUMANITY.

OVER THE COURSE OF A GENERATION, HUMANS EVOLVED INTO ANIMAL-LIKE FORMS, AND SOME EVEN BEGAN TO DEVELOP EXTRA-ORDINARY ABILITIES: *SUPERPOWERS*.

THOUGH THE COURSE OF HISTORY UNFOLDED MUCH LIKE OUR OWN, THOSE WITH POWERS BECAME AN INTEGRAL PART OF SOCIETY AND CULTURE. TODAY'S MILITARIES, POLICE FORCES AND STATE AGENCIES INCLUDE *HEROES*: JUGGERNAUTS OF JUSTICE, AS MUCH CELEBRITIES AS THEY ARE AGENTS OF THE LAW. THE LINE BETWEEN "COP" AND "CAPE" IS NOT A BLURRY ONE—IT'S NONEXISTENT.

BUT NOT EVERYONE WITH POWERS BECOMES A HERO.

SOME LEAD NORMAL LIVES, USING THEIR POWERS FOR LITTLE MORE THAN PARTY TRICKS. OTHERS USE THEM TO BOLSTER THEIR CAREERS. STILL OTHERS, HOWEVER, OPPOSE THE HEROES: AS VIGILANTES, AS CRIMINALS, AND AS *VILLAINS*.

SOME CHOOSE THE TITLE FOR THEMSELVES; OTHERS HAVE THE APPELLATION THRUST UPON THEM. REGARDLESS OF HOW THEY COME BY IT, THE BRUSH OF VILLAINY TARS ANY THAT ACT AGAINST THE ESTABLISHMENT—OR EVEN SPEAK UP TOO LOUDLY.

ONE ORGANIZATION, KNOWN AS "THE *KORPS*," HAS TAKEN UP THE BANNER OF VILLAINY WITH PRIDE. DONNING PINK VISORS RUMORED TO CONTROL THEIR MINDS, THESE NE'ER-DO-WELLS APPEAL TO THOSE LEFT BEHIND AND SHUNNED BY SOCIETY BY OFFERING SAFETY, STABILITY AND SELF-DETERMINATION. IF THESE DEVIANTS GET THEIR WAY, SOME DAY EVERYONE WILL BE FREE.

ALL THEY HAVE TO DO IS CHANGE THE WORLD—ONE MIND AT A TIME.

BEHIND THE CHARACTERS

STARSHADE IS A YOUNG AGENT OF THE SUPERVILLAINOUS KORPS. TAKEN IN OFF THE STREET AND RECENTLY CLEARED FOR FIELD WORK, THE COTTONTAIL PRIMARILY HANDLES LOW-LEVEL INFILTRATION AND HARASSMENT OPERATION AGAINST BILLIONAIRES, CORPORATIONS, AND SUPERHERO ORGANIZATIONS. CAPABLE OF LIMITED SHORT-RANGE LINE-OF-SIGHT TELEPORTATION, SHE IS A RELATIVE UNKNOWN IN THE SUPERHERO WORLD.

SHE DEBUTED IN THE NOVEL *"CRYSTALLIZATION,"* BY *RUNA FJORD*.

SLATE IS A VETERAN HERO AND PREMIER MEMBER OF THE STATE-LEVEL TEXAS PROTECTORATE ASSEMBLY. A MID-LEVEL HEAVY, THE PERCHERON POSSESSES SUPERNATURAL STRENGTH AND TOUGHNESS. AS PART OF THE DALLAS SUPERHERO TEAM THE PEGASUS PHALANX, SLATE HAS SPENT A DECADE FIGHTING CRIME AND PROTECTING THE CITY.

SLATE DEBUTED IN THE NOVEL *"CRYSTALLIZATION"* BY *RUNA FJORD*, WHERE THE REASON FOR AND CONSEQUENCES OF THE HERO'S ACTIONS UNFOLD.

VOLTA, CALLSIGN 'REDLINE,' IS INFAMOUS ACROSS THE WESTERN UNITED STATES FOR HER MERCILESS FIGHTING STYLE, AND HER VENDETTA AGAINST MANY HERO GROUPS. A ONE-TIME HERO-IN-TRAINING AND ABUSED TRANS CHILD OF EVANGELIST BILLIONAIRES, THE RED WOLF'S CLOSETED FLOUNDERING ATTRACTS A KORPS DEEP-COVER AGENT SCOUTING FOR FRESH TALENT IN LONELY TRAINEES. VOLTA JUDGES 'CAPES' ON AN EXACTING MORAL GRADIENT – AND DELIGHTS IN BEATING DOWN THOSE WHO FALL SHORT.

SHE DEBUTED IN THE NOVEL *"INDUCTION"* BY *SYNTAX TAKES*.

MABEL GREYSMOKE IS A RECENTLY FIELD-APPROVED KORPS AGENT WITH TIES TO THE MAGICAL AND MYSTICAL, WHICH GIVES HER THE POWER OF SMOKESHAPING. THIS SKILL ALLOWS THE PUMA TO TAKE ON A VAPOROUS FORM, AND PRODUCE AND CONTROL THE FORM AND DENSITY OF SMOKE, FROM HAZE TO SOLID, SUPERNATURALLY-DENSE OBSIDIAN. KNOWN FOR HER LOVE OF THEATRICS, DEEP DEVOTION TO HER CHOSEN FAMILY, AND HER RECKLESS ABANDON, MABEL JOINS THE FRAY IN A SUPPORT ROLE TO TRY AND LIMIT HER ABILITY TO FIND TROUBLE.

MABEL DEBUTED IN THE NOVEL *"GREYSMOKE RISING: THE MAGICIAN,"* BY *MABEL GREYSMOKE*.

———————————————— 8 ————————————————

MADDY GILLESPIE WAS UNTIL RECENTLY A RELUCTANT SECOND-GENERATION HERO; THE TELEKINETIC YOUNG SHEEP-BEAR WAS PRESSURED INTO THE CAREER AS A TEEN, AND CYNICALLY DEPLOYED BY HER BOSSES AS A DIVERSITY MASCOT AFTER COMING OUT AS TRANS. DISGUSTED BY LEARNING THEIR FATHER'S TRUE LEGACY OF ABUSE AND BRUTALITY AS A GOVERNMENT-BACKED HERO, THEY DEFECTED TO THE KORPS, WHERE THE UNCERTAIN NEW VILLAIN IS STILL LOOKING FOR THEIR NICHE.

MADDY DEBUTED IN THE SHORT STORY *"CHAMPION,"* BY *GRACE DUNLOP*.

———————————————— 8 ————————————————

ELLEN FOXPAW, ANOTHER VETERAN HERO, DEFECTED TO THE KORPS'S SIDE WHEN THEY OFFERED A BETTER LIFE FOR HER TWIN SISTER, VIXIE. THOUGH SHE STILL HARBORS MISTRUST FOR THE SHADOWY ORGANIZATION, THIS PUN-POWERED VULPINE TURNCOAT HAS FOUND A CADRE OF CLOSE FRIENDS AMONG THE VILLAINOUS RANKS OF THE KORPS.

ELLEN AND VIXIE'S KORPS CAREER BEGAN IN THE NOVELLA *"A SUPER VILLAIN KORPSIGIN STORY,"* BY *VIXIE FOXPAW-MOONDEW*.

———————————————— 8 ————————————————

HIRED TO REPLACE ELLEN FOXPAW AS THE STAR OF THE EVERYONE'S HERO ASSOCIATION, **STRONG** IS A DECEPTIVELY CLEVER FIGHTER. BLESSED WITH SUPERNATURAL STRENGTH AND TOUGHNESS, THE BULL ALSO WEARS A HIGH-TECH SUIT DESIGNED TO COUNTER AND DISABLE OTHER SUPERS' POWERS, GIVING HIM A NASTY EDGE IN COMBAT.

STRONG DEBUTED IN THE SHORT STORY *"A STRONG FOE,"* BY *VIXIE FOXPAW-MOONDEW* – AND THE THREAT HE POSES HAS ONLY GROWN SINCE!

ELLEN WAS THE FIRST OF THE CHARACTERS THAT I DID SOME PRACTICE SKETCHES OF.

PART OF THE EARLY WORK FOR PRODUCING THE COMIC WAS NAILING DOWN THE CHARACTER DESIGNS. I'D HAD A LITTLE BIT OF EXPERIENCE DRAWING MABEL AND VOLTA ALREADY, BUT STRONG AND ELLEN WERE COMPLETELY NEW FOR ME. THERE WERE ALSO A FEW CHARACTERS LIKE THE COLOR GUARD MEMBERS THAT ONLY APPEARED IN A HANDFUL OF PANELS THAT I FELT OUT AS I WENT ALONG.

BEHIND THE SCENES

ONCE THE DESIGNS WERE REALLY STARTING TO LOOK LIKE SOMETHING, I MOVED ON TO THE THUMBNAILING OF THE INDIVIDUAL PAGES AND PANELS, BUT NONE OF IT WOULD HAVE BEEN DOABLE WITHOUT THE VARIOUS REFERENCES AND INPUT FROM THE LOVELY WRITERS OF THESE OC'S!

I THINK IF I HAD TO CHOSE A FAVORITE CHARACTER TO DRAW DURING THIS WHOLE PROCESS IT'D PROBABLY BE MABEL. WITH THE FLAPS OF CLOTHING AND SMOKE TRAILS, CAPTURING HER MOVEMENT WAS ALWAYS A LOT OF FUN FOR ME.

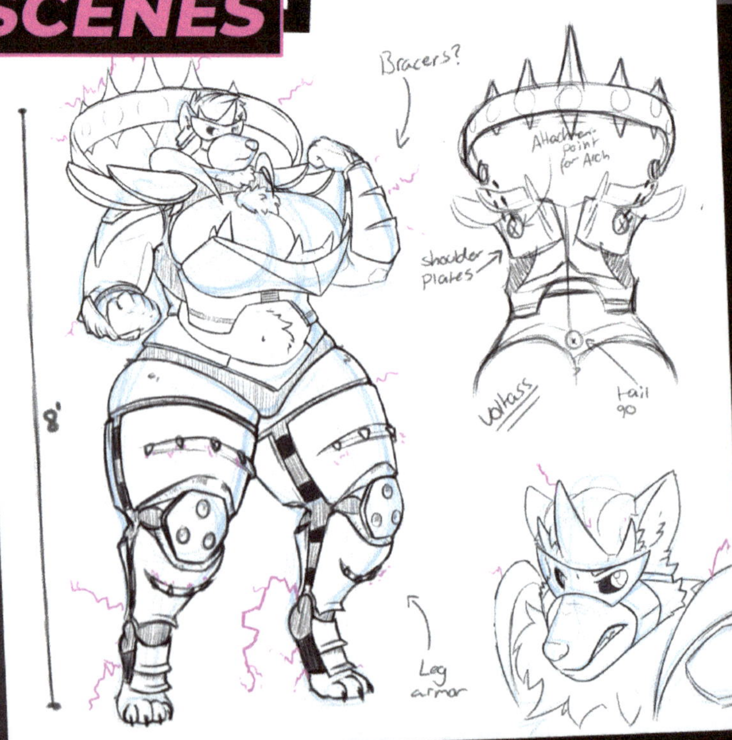

M
A
D
D
Y